TALL, DARK, AND GRUMPY

EVIE ROSE

Copyright © 2024 by Evie Rose

All rights reserved.

No part of this book may be reproduced in any form or by any electronic or mechanical means, including information storage and retrieval systems, without written permission from the author, except for the use of brief quotations in a book review.

This story is a work of fiction. Names, characters, places, and incidents are the product of the author's imagination or are used fictitiously. Any resemblance to actual events, locales, or persons, living or dead, is coincidental.

Cover: © 2024 by Evie Rose. Images under licence from Deposit Photos.

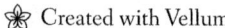 Created with Vellum

1

CASSIE

Tonight, I am going to lose my V-card.

Probably.

I'm telling myself that this doesn't have anything to do with my gorgeous new boss who has awakened my previously snoozing libido. I'm just at a bar with my housemates, like a sane person, instead of working all night with Mr Blackwood. Again.

I tug my dress down over my bottom. Next to me, my three housemates are giggling.

"Oh my god, we should have shots!" exclaims Julie.

"I can get them," I say eagerly. I'm keen for my housemates to like me, and help me find someone to spend the night with. Teach me their slutty ways, and to like boys in their twenties. So far all I can see is guys who are like baby dolphins: all smooth chests, wet-look hair, and disturbingly shiny white teeth.

Eeeee-eee, throw me a fish!

Not my thing.

I'm more of a bear girl. I like men who are big, slightly terrifying, six-foot-three, grizzly, dark-brown hair, blue eyes... No. I'm not thinking about Mr Blackwood this evening. I will learn to like dolphins, and be part of the conversation without being awkward. Buying more alcohol is a rare social situation I'm certain I can manage.

"My new boss—"

Polly and Tamara catch each other's eyes and collapse into laughter, chinking their glasses and drinking.

"What?" I ask.

"Nothing, nothing." Tamara smirks.

Polly whispers something into Tamara's ear and I get an unwelcome sinking feeling in my tummy. I don't fit with them. They're effortlessly wearing their fashionable dresses, but I look like a sack of potatoes in almost the exact same thing. I swallow my discomfort.

"Well, my new boss—"

They giggle again and clink glasses.

"He gave me a pay raise, so we can celebrate." A very generous pay raise to go with the insane hours he expects me to work. Mr Blackwood is new to London, and he took over the Esher mafia which owns the company I work for as an accountant. I'm now the head of finance, which is crazy given I'm twenty-two.

"Sure," Polly says, knocking back the last of her flute of champagne.

"Don't go anywhere, I'll be back with drinks!" I say brightly.

Julie isn't listening, she's looking around the room. Polly and Tamara are deep in conversation, leaning together to whisper.

I make my way to the bar. It's quiet for a Friday. Well, I assume it is. I'm not great with this sort of thing.

But I'm having a good time. I am.

Probably.

I am not thinking about Mr Blackwood and what he's doing tonight after I said earlier that I had somewhere to be, and couldn't work late. I am not wishing I was at work, called into his office, or suddenly sensing his dark and grouchy presence behind me before he growls something like, "That light isn't bright enough, stop straining your eyes," or "Sit up straight."

At the bar I glance around while I wait to be served. A few men catch my eye despite my being plain, even in this short cream dress. I have long mid-brown hair and pale blue eyes, and I'm curvy. Not special.

One guy tries to hold my gaze though. Not my type. I look down at my hands and I'm thankful when a barman approaches.

"Four shots, please."

"What sort?" he says impatiently.

"I, uh." I have no idea. Alcoholic ones.

I glance around for inspiration. Across the bar, there's a group of women—all together, no one left out of the group, I note—drinking shots. One is a bit older, and the other three are all younger. The older woman has grey in her hair and is heavier around the middle, but still attractive. The younger women are full of confidence. A mother and daughters' night out, I realise with a pang of jealousy.

It's not that I don't get on with my mother. I call her every week. We talk about scintillating topics like the weather, the health of my brother, and my dad's bird watching. Sometimes she tells me about my aunt's bunions, and I pretend to know what those are, because I *really* don't want to ask. Or know.

My interactions with my parents are more surface than hand cream. I wish I had a relationship like those women, who are laughing together. One of the younger women hugs the older woman tight and whispers something in her ear that makes the older woman smile.

"Those multi-coloured shots," I say, pointing at the women. "I'll have those."

The barman looks unimpressed. "The rainbow flavoured vodka round."

"Yep. Seems fun." I am upbeat.

At least it's deliberate this time. The vending machine had run out of normal, extra-safe condoms, so I bought the novelty selection.

Fruit flavoured. Neon coloured.

The plum one is *purple*.

What man wants their dick to look like an eggplant emoji?

And this is why I'm single. I guess vegetables are as close as I'll ever get.

Never mind, flavoured *vodka* will be great. My housemates will think I'm cool, and include me in their jokes. They'll give me the secret to attracting an experienced, hot man who will blow my mind and take my virginity. Using one of my emoji condoms.

The barman pours seven shots into little heavy-bottomed glasses and lines them up on the bar. Ooof. Okay. Seven shots for four of us. This is fine. One for me, and the other girls can take two each.

"Are you adding these to your tab?" the barman asks, and I nod.

"It's wild to me that people don't run off without paying their tab," I say conversationally as he checks me against the photo driving licence I gave as a guarantee.

"Trust and consequences." He shrugs. "It's common in Blackwood-controlled parts of London. We've only been able to do it since the takeover, and haven't had any trouble. Because who'd want to mess with a Blackwood?"

Well, it depends on what you mean by mess, because I wouldn't mind getting messy with my boss. I also feel a silly glow of pride that he has increased security in his territory, but agree politely rather than over-share that Mr Blackwood is my boss.

I turn to the table where I left my housemates, but find it empty. Odd. It takes me a moment to scan around the bar to where the little dance floor of the bar has filled up... with three familiar girls in tight dresses.

Oh fiddlesticks. They didn't wait for drinks and now they aren't looking my way at all. How am I going to get the shots over in one journey? I can't leave them unattended, as I've heard about girls having their drinks spiked in London and Blackwood territory or not, I'm not risking that.

"Are you going to do all those shots?" a voice asks from behind me.

I swing around to find a man who was on the other side of the bar looking me up and down, lingering on the neckline of my dress where my breasts are far more on show than usual. He's not even subtle and his regard is like a cheap plastic raincoat on my bare skin.

He has light-brown hair and is wearing a white shirt that doesn't fit him somehow, and has creases in odd places as though it's just out of a packet. Well. I say man. I suppose he has been through puberty, but he's not a man like Mr Blackwood is a man. He's shiny, thin, and new where Mr Blackwood is solid, rough, and life-worn.

And while I said my aim for tonight was to sleep with someone, I instantly know this man is not it. I prefer the idea of a more experienced man. Taller. Bright blue eyes. Darker hair.

Gah, I'm thinking of my boss, *again*.

"I'm sharing them." I hop up onto a stool. "My friend will be over in a minute."

"Mind if I join you? I wasn't having any luck getting the barman's attention over there, but I think you might be my lucky charm." The man smiles and it's so oily you could fry eggs with him.

I glance over at my housemates, who are dancing with some other young men now. The dolphin man lounges at the bar next to me, and out of the corner of my eye I can see him checking out my chunky thighs.

Ohhhh noo. I tug at the hem of my dress again, and wish I hadn't listened when Julie said I should wear it.

The man edges closer, and I realise he's going to speak to me again. Yanking my purse open, I pull out my phone.

"Are you sure they're coming?" the man asks, a sarky tone to his question.

"Yes," I lie. I check over my shoulder at my housemates, who still aren't looking at me. They've probably forgotten I exist.

I'm on my own, stuck at the bar with seven vodka shots and a man I'm feeling increasingly uncomfortable with.

I open my messages, press the top contact blindly, hyper-aware of leaning away from the man next to me. Tapping something out, I hit send before my brain catches up with what I'm doing.

CASSIE

Hi

And I realise I've messaged my *boss*.

"If I were you, I'd just down those shots and have a *good time* with who's here," the man says suggestively, as I stare in horror at my phone.

What have I done? Can I…? Cold horror trickles down my spine.

If I delete the message, it will still show up as having been sent and then deleted. Mr Blackwood is going to know.

"If you're short of company, you can join me," the man continues. "Who are you texting?"

"My bo…boyfriend." The word just pops out.

I nearly said boss. That's even more tragic than a made-up boyfriend, isn't it? Texting your boss on a Friday night? Never mind that we text often. Exciting conversations like, "Come to my office," and "I've finished the report you asked for".

"He's stood you up on a Friday night, huh?" the man scoffs.

"No." I can't manage this intruder, and I cannot fix that I messaged my boss. I'm a failure. Can this night get any worse?

Alcohol is supposed to improve everything, isn't it? I reach out and grab one of the shots. It's a blue the colour of Mr Blackwood's eyes—how appropriate—and I knock it back in one. The vodka burns my throat, and I cough.

"That's it!" The man next to me laughs.

I ignore him, slam down the glass and type "Sorry" into the messaging app. Then I stop. Because how many times over the last month has Mr Blackwood messaged me at all hours? Sometimes early in the morning, as though he can't sleep.

He probably hasn't even seen it. He'll be having a

sophisticated dinner with a blonde woman who talks to him about quantum physics or something. Or makes him laugh.

He won't be looking out for a message from me. I bet on a Friday night he—

The tick changes colour, indicating he's seen the message.

Oh. Shit.

That was super quick. I didn't think he... Scrap that. I didn't think. I felt threatened by the man next to me, and my body messaged the person I contact most often. And, if I'm honest, the person who makes me feel safe. Mr Blackwood.

But it's okay. He'll ignore it. I glance down at my phone.

BOSS

...

The three balls bounce. My heart stops. He hasn't just seen my message casually. Whatever I thought I could get away with, I was wrong.

Because my boss is texting me back.

2

VITO

ONE MONTH EARLIER

I really should have just killed everyone to take over this London mafia. Sitting at the head of the long boardroom table and as the head of finance drones on over surprisingly good presentation slides, I consider rewinding the clock. This mafia territory and all the businesses I've acquired are a mess, and I think at least some of the staff are still loyal to either the Geracis or the Newhavens before them. I should just dispose of them all, and be done.

But it's impossible to tell who is lying, because after two take-overs of Esher in two years, everyone in the meeting is visibly nervous, or sweating, or both.

"And you see the projections..." Mr Hathaway mutters some numbers. "So the need for investment is critical."

Just like that, I'm engaged with this again, because there's a discrepancy, and that's why I called this meeting. To give Hathaway enough rope to hang himself with.

"You said there has been stagnation in the last two

years," I snap. "Those slides show an increase. Which is true?"

"Mr Blackwood, I—"

"Which is correct?" Fury solidifies in my chest.

"I'm sorry," he says, "there must be some mistake in the numbers."

"You're giving me wrong numbers," I state, my voice lowering to the calm soft pitch that everyone in Milan knew to fear. But these men don't know me well yet.

"Not me, I apologise." He swallows, but there's something underhand about him. I don't trust it.

"Who made the mistake?" I lounge back in my chair. I'm interested to see how this will play out.

"My Junior Assistant Accounting Clerk produced these slides." His gaze is too steady, and his forehead is beaded with sweat. Something is being hidden from me.

"Bring in whoever made them."

"But—"

"Now." I'm not sure if he knows how close to death he is. But perhaps he does, because after only a second's hesitation he scurries out of the room.

We all wait.

I drum my fingers on the table, irritation spiking through me. Of all the fucking stupidity, I had to give myself this problem. I was *fine* in Milan. Absolutely *fine*. I should never have returned to London, because it hasn't sealed the gaping hole in my chest. It hasn't made me less lonely.

The worst part is that the eldest of my two identical brothers, Rafe, has a new wife he's sickeningly in love with. Sev transparently has a crush on a woman, but becomes tight-lipped when asked who. I'm the third kingpin in London with the same face, but a stranger. I have no one.

This whole bloody enterprise—and it has been bloody in parts, despite my having gone about the take-over legitimately—was a mistake.

The glass door swooshes open, and the curvy shape of a young woman draws my eye.

"Good morning!"

The air is sucked from my lungs.

I stare.

The girl—and she is no more than a girl compared to me—Hathaway has brought to take the blame, is the most beautiful thing I've ever seen.

Renaissance paintings? Rubbish. Roman architecture? Dull. The Italian sunshine? Paltry.

This girl's soft, closed-mouth smile as she flits her gaze around the room is stunning. Her pale blue eyes are gentle like a cloud coyly drifting over the summer sky. Her brunette hair—was ever there a word so inadequate?—shines, a tendril falling over her cheek and the rest in a loose knot at the back of her head. My god, I want to take down her hair and see it spread across my pillow as I thrust into her and make her mine more than I want my next breath.

Dressed in a neat pair of loose trousers and a scoop-necked top in a navy that contrasts with her eyes, making them seem even paler blue, she's professional yet elegant. As she shifts from foot to foot, I notice her practical but worn flat shoes. But even her carefully chosen appropriate office wear doesn't disguise that she's got a body made for sin.

She must be more than a head shorter than me, but she's all curves. Her breasts would be the perfect handful, her hips were made to be held as I take her from behind.

There aren't words for how lovely she is, or not in English there aren't. A stream of sensual Italian phrases run through my mind, accompanying imaginings of her naked body. Beneath me, on top of me, her face creased with ecstasy.

"This is Miss Meadows." Hathaway jerks me unpleasantly from my all-too-pleasant thoughts and back to reality, where I see that she's nervous, but smiling cheerfully through it. So sweet.

This young woman...

I don't allow my expression to change, my features steady in a dark scowl.

There are pivot points in life. My first kill. Leaving London to go to Milan. First territory. First million. One billion. The day Miss Meadows walked into my boardroom and stole my heart. Or rather, that previously stony organ bounced up like a puppy and threw itself over to the Junior Assistant Accounting Clerk.

My *employee*.

She was probably born around the time I took over the territory on the outskirts of Milan when I was twenty. I ought to be disgusted with that thought, but I can't be. I can only want.

Amore mio dolce. My sweet love.

Everyone in the room is waiting for me to say something, I realise.

I clear my throat, and Miss Meadows widens her smile.

"Did you make these slides?"

She nods.

"Use your words, Miss Meadows." I'm coming across as severe. It's been too long, and I suppose I'm broken now. Unable to express any gentler feeling, even as it overflows, surging out of my ribcage.

"Yes." Her voice is sweet and higher than I expected,

and it makes her seem even younger. Usually, I prefer women my age, but this girl is irresistible.

"And the data shown in the presentation, where is it from?"

"I, er..." Her gaze slides to the side to her boss, Mr Hathaway.

"Look at me," I bark and her chin snaps back, her eyes meeting mine. "Where is it from?"

"I ran the analysis myself."

"And is it correct?"

"Well, it can't be," Hathaway blusters.

"Shut up." I don't move my focus from the girl who has captured my attention, and I suspect, my heart. "Is it right, Miss Meadows?"

There's a long, fraught silence. She blinks several times, the delicate fan of her lashes shadowing her cheek.

"I believe so," she whispers, smiling nervously.

The head of finance is a treacherous *coglione*. I'd be angrier, except he brought me *her*. I might not have known that the creature who could touch my soul existed if she hadn't walked into this room.

This girl...

She's been here alive, for what—twenty years maybe?— and I haven't known her. I've lived forty fucking years missing out.

I wonder if this is why I've felt so lonely. I've never lacked company, and I returned to London to see if spending time with my brothers would help fill the void. But now, it's as though she's a bright furnace and I'm broken glass. She softens all my edges, reforming me into... Okay, I'll always be a demanding *bastardo*, but for her, I'd melt.

I take a few minutes to ask her more about the company's financial situation, and the more I ask, the more confident she becomes as she recognises I'm not going to brush her off. She knows her stuff, and I think is used to being ignored.

"Miss Meadows says you're lying, Mr Hathaway," I say eventually. I don't take my eyes off Miss Meadows.

She lets out a terrified squeak. "No! I—"

I put one hand up to silence her, and good girl that she is, she cuts immediately. "And I'm inclined to believe her. You think I wasn't aware that you were skimming off the profits from my predecessor?"

Admittedly, it was a hunch. But Miss Meadows has confirmed it.

"That's a serious and unfounded accusation." Hathaway tries to sound authoritative, and fails.

"It's also true."

"Tony," I say softly to my second-in-command.

"Capo Mandamento." He replies with my honorific rather than my name and several people shift uncomfortably. Apparently, it's not done in London to admit you're a mafia boss. But it is by me. My capo bastone, brought from Milan, steps forward from where he's been standing at the back of the room.

"Tony, take Mr Hathaway to retire to *Naples*." I've always thought it was unfair to use Naples as the code for hell. I quite like Naples and have a villa just outside the city. I'd love to take Miss Meadows there one day... Except that's as likely as Hathaway actually going to Naples rather than being murdered by Tony.

"I can help you!" Mr Hathaway protests as Tony quietly and efficiently removes him from the room. Everyone else watches, but I can't look away from Miss Meadows. She's stunning. She'd look even better with my baby swelling her midriff.

The door shuts behind Hathaway, and some of the tension flows with him.

"Now, Miss Meadows."

She pinkens, but there's steel in that adorably short spine of hers. Her chin tilts up. "Yes, Mr Blackwood."

I love the way she says my name. It would be even better if she said it while on my cock. I lean forwards to disguise the untimely turgidity in my trousers.

There's a muffled sound from outside the room, followed by an audible, "No, please!"

I sigh. Tony is reliable and efficient, but sometimes he lacks finesse.

There's a shot, and a thud.

"Oh my god," a woman on the left whispers.

Turning, I glare at her.

"I don't like being lied to, and I don't like incompetence," I say.

There's a murmur of submissive agreement. No one wants to be the next to be removed.

To Miss Meadows, I say, "You're the new head of finance."

She gapes.

"You can do it, can't you?"

Her shoulders go back, and while she's shaking, I admire her courage. The last person in her job role was shot, and she doesn't know that she is under my protection now. "Yes, Mr Blackwood."

"Good. Take over the presentation, please. Since you prepared it, I'm sure you can."

Her pretty, pale eyes go wide and there's a moment when I think she might run away. Her gaze flicks to the rest of the people in the room, as though for approval, and her expression drops as she finds nothing there but fear.

"You're not talking to them." Her head snaps around. "Just talk to me, Miss Meadows."

"Yes, of course, Mr Blackwood."

She works for me. I'm going to exploit that shamelessly. I'll be her work daddy. Whatever she needs. I'd also be her lover, her husband, her everything, but there's no chance of that.

Whether she likes it or not, I'm going to nurture her. First, I'm going to find out everything about her, then, I'll give her everything she's ever wanted.

I thought I'd be ignoring this company? Just goes to show what an idiot I was only an hour ago. I'll be working night and day to ensure Miss Meadows has a long, happy, fulfilling life.

There's only one thing I want to achieve now: care for amore mio dolce. My forbidden girl.

3

CASSIE

It takes a while for my pulse to return to normal when I stumble back from the meeting. There's shock and hushed disbelief as I hang onto my desk, trying to feel the chair and my back and centre myself. I can't quite believe that just happened. There's a blur of emotions in me, and they're all tinged with the electric blue of my boss' eyes.

I think Mr Blackwood killed my old boss and promoted me into his role.

Me. A twenty-two-year-old who understands spreadsheets better than social dynamics.

I can see the logic of numbers. They have rules written down, whereas people have rules that no one can tell me what they are, so I always muck them up. And in this case, it seems to have been fatal.

Mr Blackwood has put his trust in me, and I'm equal parts terrified and exhilarated.

But even having seen photos of Mr Blackwood, and the other two Blackwood triplet kingpins, *Vito* Blackwood is different. In person, he's an Egyptian god. He's part black snake, part blue jay, and all muscled, bulky man, his hair touched with silver as though he's permanently in the moonlight.

He is hot, and for the first time in my life, my body appears to have awoken to that. I've never thought much about men. I wasn't boy-crazy like some of the girls at school, and I didn't sleep around at university. I didn't sleep with anyone, I never wanted to.

But Vito Blackwood? Oof.

The fact he's ruthless, has piercing eyes that gleam with dark knowledge, and is my boss, only makes this feeling all the more forbidden and tempting.

Oh, and if I don't do well with my new job, he might have me killed.

Drawing in a deep breath, I flick on my computer and open my pretty, decorated notebook, and start writing a to-do list. This promotion is huge, and I'm determined to show my boss that even if I'm as bad at dealing with people as he is—though less murderous—I am competent at my job.

I'm several pages through, pulling numbers from a spreadsheet and jotting them down, when I notice that everything has gone quiet around me.

The back of my neck prickles and nervously, I begin to turn.

My boss is looming over my shoulder, his square jaw only inches away, as he leans to examine my workspace.

A squeak escapes me.

In my small cubicle, he seems even bigger than from a distance in the board meeting. Not because he's scary. Or, not only because he's scary.

He makes me feel tiny, like a doll. I am not classic doll shaped. I'm curvy, and suddenly I'm hyperaware of how I'm small and slight and soft because he's big and hard and bulky.

"That's a tiny working space." He glares at my desk, potted fern, pink pens, and the cute sticker-covered notebook I have open. "How do you get anything done?"

Ack. He doesn't like my plants? I stop myself from dragging them protectively to me. They're my friends, especially the one with the triangular purple leaves.

"I do most things on my computer," I say brightly, and it's true. "I don't print things unnecessarily, so it's big enough."

"You'll strain your eyes, Miss Meadows." His brow darkens and he slowly regards my space, scanning from left to right. "And this isn't appropriate for your new role. Come with me."

I half expect him to lead me to my boss' office, a glass walled section much larger than any of the cubicles on the main floor with most of the employees. But he doesn't, and I follow him to the elevator, where he jabs the button to the top level of the building. I stand beside him awkwardly, not knowing what to say. My chest tightens as the doors open. Since Mr Blackwood took over, this floor has been rearranged into sleek meeting rooms and offices, with a large central space with a glass roof that could be used as a dance floor, or for tenpin bowling, if you had a death wish.

Which I do not.

"That's my office," Mr Blackwood says unnecessarily, as we pass enormous opaque glass doors and come to another set beyond. "And this is yours."

He throws open the door and stands back. My jaw must have a technical problem, because for the second time today my mouth falls open and refuses to close.

This office is amazing. It's enormous, with floor-to-ceiling windows that look out over the London skyline, hazy white clouds and blue sky stained with yellow sunlight. The carpet is so thick it's probably more comfortable than my mattress, the desk is huge and shiny, and has on it a computer that probably costs more than my annual rent. The conference table, sofas, and space enough to do yoga are just the icing on top. Even though I don't do yoga. Last time I tried I pulled a muscle and couldn't walk for days.

There's even a coffee machine. A coffee machine! Just for me!

"The windows face east. In the morning, you'll want to block out the light." Mr Blackwood picks up a control from the desk, and as I watch, the windows turn opaque, then become reflective, until in a few seconds they are floor-to-ceiling mirrors. And I'm staring at me, tiny, next to my extremely tall and powerful boss. He meets my gaze in the mirror.

"Does that meet with your approval?"

I nod. I didn't realise glass could do that.

"Thank you."

His brows pinch together, and he takes a breath. For a second, I'm convinced he's going to say something. But he doesn't, and neither does he move.

"I'll justify the trust you've put in me," I add earnestly, filling in the gap. I'm eager for my boss' approval.

Dropping his gaze, he turns abruptly, and walks out. No goodbye. No further comment.

And my stupid heart thuds.

The next day, I'm set up in my new office. A team of sinister looking but very polite Italian men brought all my stuff from my cubicle downstairs and all I had to do was tweak their positions. Then I started getting to grips with my new job, which was easier than it sounds because honestly, I was doing everything for my old boss except giving the presentations. The analysis, the reports, everything was written by me. I was in until late last night though, and I'm in early in the morning, determined to make a good impression.

Mr Blackwood has emailed overnight, and there are messages on my phone too. He's asking for an update by the end of the day.

When I've figured out what I need to do, I grab another coffee and when I check the time, I'm shocked to discover it's after twelve, so I unpack the sandwiches and chocolate bar I bought on my way into work, and put them at my elbow to eat while I work through lunch. I unwrap the chocolate first, because why not, and get back into the spreadsheet.

"Miss Meadows."

My head snaps up, mid mouthful. Mr Blackwood is standing in the entrance to my office, having magically stealthed his way in and I am stuffing my face with chocolate.

"Mr Black..." Oh god. I cover my mouth and cringe. So much for looking professional.

"You're eating at your desk, Miss Meadows."

My heart skips a beat, not getting the memo that he's my boss and not a sabre-toothed tiger.

"Yes. I was keen to keep working on..." I gesture at my screen.

His eyes narrow. "What are you eating?"

Oh no... Not this. Please not the "eat less sugar and you'll be slimmer". I can't cope. Or rather, I can, but not without risking being shot for shouting at my boss.

"A sandwich and a small treat," I chirp. He cannot

murder me for eating something he doesn't approve of. This isn't a bible story. I refuse to believe it.

"You should eat more healthily."

"It's healthy," I protest. "There's—"

"That isn't good enough, Miss Meadows." He picks up my crumpled budget sandwich and scowls at it.

"Okay," I whisper. "I'll bring in food from home." Ugh, I was looking forward to buying lunch rather than making it now I've had a pay raise.

That seems to incense him even more. "No more eating lunch at your desk."

"But—"

"It's not good for you not to take a break," he interrupts in a stern voice that causes an unexpected throb in my clit. "Get up."

It shocks me so much I don't point out that most of the reason I'm working hard is because he gave me a promotion, and rise from my seat trying not to squirm.

I'm turned on by him being stern and commanding. What is wrong with me? My heart leaps as he strides around the desk and cups my elbow. He practically frog marches me out of the office, the door banging behind us. There are curious stares from the executive assistants working in the foyer as he leads me to the elevator, and out of the building.

He doesn't let go of my elbow until we're in a restaurant with white tablecloths and the best pasta I've ever eaten. Mr Blackwood grumbles about the lack of authenticity of the Italian food, questions me constantly about work, and watches me clear my plate like a hawk tracking a mouse.

Probably I shouldn't have eaten as much as I did, never mind agreeing to dessert—tiramisu—but honestly it was delicious and why should I hold back? It's not like this is a date. Though, saying that, it's not like I have any experience of dating, so what would I know?

He pays with a wedge of cash tossed onto the table that makes my eyes bulge and when we're back on the top floor, he stalks to his office without so much as a, "Hope you had a good lunch."

"Thank you," I call from the elevator where he's left me for dust.

He doesn't even turn. But he pauses, one hand on the door, and rasps, "From now on, if you need to have a working lunch, you have it with *me*."

Mr Blackwood is as good as his word. He takes me out for lunch to the Italian restaurant three days that week, usually stomping into my office or ringing about the task he gave me only a few hours before and that needs the whole day.

After the fateful Monday morning meeting, he's done nothing but growl. I don't know what level of supervision is normal in a new job like this, but I think he's checking up on me too. Usually, he phones as soon as I get into the office in the morning to check on the progress of whatever I'm working on. Then at some point during the day he'll appear at the door, or phone and say, "Come to my office, Miss Meadows," in that rough, deep voice of his. And every time my heart lifts in a silly way. I thought it was nerves at first, but... No.

On Wednesday I arrive at work with damp hair after walking in the rain, and when I'm called in to see him, he takes in my appearance and demands an explanation. I protest that I like the exercise, and it'll be dry in half an hour, but he overrules me. I end up with a chauffeur driven SUV to take me to and from work.

And I kinda like it.

On Thursday, he zeros in on my pink keyboard. And okay, yes, it was a bit dirty. I should have cleaned it, and the "a" sticks sometimes. The new ergonomic one that arrived a few hours later is easier to type on. But it's not pink.

On Friday, I don't hear from him at all except an email first thing about a report he needs by the end of the day. At quarter to five, I'm going through the last details when my neck prickles. I stroke the hairs back down, and refocus.

Then the scent of citrus and sandalwood catches at my nose and I stop typing.

It's him.

The air crackles with electric tension. I can hear him breathing. He's watching me, and he knows that I know.

But Mr Blackwood makes no movement to announce his presence.

I can't move. Creaky like the tinman, and as lacking in courage as the lion. I'm fixed in place. His gaze, now I've realised it's on me, is hot as the summer sun.

"I'm nearly done with the updated projections you asked for," I croak.

"Good." The single word is clipped. "Because I've realised the ones you sent yesterday aren't broken down by month and I need them to review over the weekend."

That snaps my head around. "By month? But you asked for quarterly!" It'll take forever to redo that.

I could bite off my tongue as my eyes meet the bright blue eyes of my billionaire kingpin boss. Oh. Shit. His eyes are a summer sky, but his expression is thunder.

"Is there a problem?"

"It's fine!" I smile. "I'll work late."

He gives a single nod. "Tell me," he begins, without a thank-you, to ask for complex details about the previous financials of the company.

The way he listens as I reply is what makes me think I'm losing my mind. Because although his brows remain low, there's an intensity in his attention that shimmers across my skin.

There must be something wrong with me, because grumpy and sour and difficult and objectively terrifying as my boss is, I think I like him. I enjoy his blue gaze on me, and the way he concentrates on me. He takes every word I say seriously.

I don't want to disappoint him. So, when we seamlessly move from what he asked about to a new topic, then another, I don't complain.

The massive pay increase doesn't hurt, and that's a good justification for why as the sun sets, turning the sky pink through the massive windows of my office, I don't mention that it's late, on a Friday.

What else do I have to do with my Friday evenings? It's not like I have a boyfriend or invitations to go partying.

By the end of a month, I've come to a conclusion: I have to lose my virginity.

Pressing my thighs together all day might be good for my inner leg muscle strength, but it's a disaster for my concentration. I might be tempted to quit, but for three things:

One, my predecessor in this role didn't leave voluntarily, shall we say, and I prefer to remain alive. Especially because it seems Mr Blackwood hates me, and considers me the cause of the permanent rain cloud above his head. That is the only rational explanation for how he grumps at me all the time.

Two, objectively, I have a great job. All the salary and benefits perks, plus some I didn't realise I needed, like regular working lunches with my thundercloud boss.

But I'd still quit, if it weren't for reason number three. Because what started as an inconvenient tendency of my heart to race whenever Mr Blackwood was around has developed into a full-blown crush.

Which is insane.

I have the world's most stupid crush on my demanding, grumpy, unreasonable, gorgeous boss. The evidence is irrefutable. I tingle under his gaze. When he scowls, I swoon. The mere sound of him saying "Miss Meadows" reverberates in my heart.

I've worked harder this month than I ever have before in my life. And what's wild is, the more growly he is, the more I respond inappropriately.

When Mr Blackwood drops by my desk, and demands, "Why are you still here?" at nine at night, my pussy twitches. I'm there because I want his approval. Because I end up wondering what he'd look like naked when he's watching me. I wonder what he'd feel like on top of me.

Or *in* me. Mmmhmm.

I gave a presentation to him and other department heads, and though during the questions he was full of quiet approval, afterwards, he pulled me aside and said, "You need to control your fidgeting."

"Of course, Mr Blackwood," I replied, but really, I thought, oh shoot. He noticed me being hot and squirmy in his presence.

I have an itch I can't satisfy.

Because of this, I desperately need a life outside of work and Mr Blackwood so that I can stop being so pathetic about my boss.

Thankfully, since I've been so busy, I haven't managed to change living circumstances. This morning, I asked my housemate Julie if I could come with them tonight when they went out, and she agreed.

There's only one small hitch: telling my boss.

It's funny, there are two types of days, I've noticed. Some days, when I arrive in the morning, there's a message from Mr Blackwood, or he calls almost immediately.

Other days, it's not until late afternoon that he'll appear at my office door, or message asking me to come to his office. It's as though some days he refrains from contacting me. Or maybe he just forgets me.

Today, it's an afternoon visit to my office with an unfeasible amount of work to be done before the weekend. I muster all my courage, and say, "I'm sorry, that's not going to be possible. I can't work late tonight."

There's a silence as thick and black as the two seconds when I was in the basement level of the building when the power went out, before the emergency lights flickered on, and I'm just as terrified.

"You can't work tonight?" he says with dangerous calm. "Why not?"

"It's a Friday evening," I point out.

"Do you not value the job I gave you?"

I break apart inside, because yes, and I value him even more. But it's because of all the unwanted, forbidden feelings he invokes in me that I *have* to go out tonight.

"Mr Blackwood, this is the first evening I haven't worked this month. You don't want me to let my friends down, do you?"

I cross my fingers for luck and for the lie.

His jaw tightens.

"Enjoy your evening, Miss Meadows," he snaps, and turning on his heel, strides out of the office.

Staring after him, my heart sinks. I'm a hopeless case. Because I suspect I'm not going to have a good evening unless it's with my boss.

4

VITO

THAT EVENING

I genuinely thought that when I moved to London to expand my mafia empire that my main problem would be my two identical triplet brothers who are already kingpins here.

But no. Not at all. It's my pocket-sized ball of sunshine employee.

Miss Cassie Meadows.

I stare at the message.

> AMORE MIO DOLCE
> Hi

My phone doesn't sound for anyone. Not my brothers, Sev and Rafe, not anyone from Milan where I've lived most of my adult life. No one interrupts me.

Except for Miss Meadows.

I turned on alerts for her, because I have to know whenever she contacts me. Whenever she's thinking of me, I want to relish that, even if it's only because she's responding to messages about work.

She's never initiated a conversation.

Until now.

One word, on a Friday night she insisted on having off and I agreed against my every instinct. I grip my phone as though it might run away. I somehow fear if I stop looking at her one precious word, it will disappear.

"What is it?" Sev asks from the other white leather sofa. We've spent the evening together discussing London mafia politics, and he's been trying to convince me to join the London Mafia Syndicate. I invited him over at the last minute, and he's been a good sport about my bad mood.

I ignore him, and try to figure out what to reply.

"Are you even listening to me?"

"No," I reply, and type out a reply on my phone.

VITO

Hello.

For a second, that's all I can think to say. She says hi, I respond. I will be at the end of the phone anytime she needs. The typing dots appear, then stop. Then start again.

She's talking to me outside of work. Why?

"Fuck's sake, Vito," Sev grumbles, half annoyed, half amused, which is his natural state. All of the Blackwood brothers', to be honest. "You've been away for twenty years and now you're back, and we've hardly seen you in a month. You invite me over for the evening, barely talk, and now you're on your phone."

"Vaffanculo."

"You can swear at me, but you know I'm right." Sev shrugs.

And the infuriating thing is, that's probably true.

AMORE MIO DOLCE

Soz

I mean, sorry.

No, I don't. You always message me in the evenings. Not sorry.

VITO

Is everything alright, Miss Meadows?

"Who are you messaging so secretively?" Sev swirls whisky in his glass. Disgusting smoky paint stripper. Wine or beer are so much better.

"It's just work." And I'm not sure whether that's a lie. But I know I wish it were.

AMORE MIO DOLCE

Yeeaaahhhsssss ish

"Work?" Sev's voice comes from behind me, and I jolt. "But you message her on a Friday night, name her 'amore mio dolce' in your phone, and address her as Miss Meadows. Your sweet love. What is she? Your dungeon mistress?"

"Something like that," I mutter, and Sev barks out a laugh. "And get her name out of your mouth, stronzo."

Unease is snaking through my veins. This doesn't feel like the cautious, shy Miss Meadows I'm familiar with. Something has lowered her inhibitions dangerously.

VITO

Are you drunk?

AMORE MIO DOLCE

It's a FRIDAY. I'm trying to live a little.

Having shots. Why not?

My blood turns to ice. Who is there with her? I know

she isn't close to her family since she let slip that she only phones her mother once a week. She mentioned a house share, and her nose wrinkled as she did. Does she have someone to take care of her while she's drunk?

Fuck. That someone is me. It must be me, because no one else will take care of her as well as I will.

> **VITO**
> Where are you?

> **AMORE MIO DOLCE**
> Sorry, this was a mistake. Worst evening ever.

> **VITO**
> Where are you?

Desperation pounds in my head.

I don't even know whether she's in my territory. What if she's in Essex or someplace?

"Vito, don't worry," Sev says soothingly, still looking over my shoulder. "I've got software you can put on her phone so you can keep track of her. It's reliable. And I can probably find her current position if you give me her phone number."

"What? No." I'm distracted, attention split between what my crazy brother is saying and waiting as the notification dots bounce. What is my brother saying? "That's stalking... No."

"Nothing wrong with keeping an eye on people," Sev mutters.

> **AMORE MIO DOLCE**
> To go with the worst boss, ever.

I'm hit from all sides by fucking terrible thoughts and

realisations. My heart is pounding and there's a tightness in my chest. No, a pain. My hand shakes as I put the phone down, so Sev can't see anything else she says.

Is this some joke? She thinks I'm a bad boss? I don't understand. I've tried to take care of her. A huge salary, proper food so she's healthy, ensuring she doesn't slouch and damage her back, the prestigious office right next to mine. Alright, there's some self interest in that I want her close to me.

My brother is saying whatever the fuck he says in that goddamn drawl that's exactly like mine except without an Italian accent. I can't hear him over the ringing in my ears.

Worst boss ever?

Whatever she thinks, there is one person I'm not listening to. "Shut up, Sev."

VITO
Location. Now.

AMORE MIO DOLCE
At a bar.

VITO
Which bar?

AMORE MIO DOLCE
Dunno

VITO
Which bar, Miss Meadows? Tell me now.

AMORE MIO DOLCE
Keep your hair on

VITO
I am. You're turning it grey.

> **AMORE MIO DOLCE**
> You'd think they'd have a "you are here" sign for drunk people.
>
> I'll ask the barman.

> **VITO**
> No.

> **AMORE MIO DOLCE**
> Why not?

Because she's the most beautiful woman in the world, and she'll have men swarming around her. They'll be trying to get into her knickers. Maybe the barman, or anyone in the bar. Panic surges. I can't let her be taken advantage of if she's drunk in a bar. She sounds drunk. She's around *drunk people*. Anything could happen to her.

> **VITO**
> Send me a pin of your location.

I hold my breath. Part of me is convinced she will ignore me, or refuse. One minute ticks by, then two. I have to inhale. I force myself to.

"I use it to keep tabs on... Someone important," Sev is wittering on, trying to show me some app or another. I give him a death look and he rolls his eyes. "What is the point of being a mafia boss if you're not going to use shady techniques?"

"Because..." I can't express why I have to play it straight with Miss Meadows. *Cassie*. God, I really shouldn't allow myself to think of her like that. After all, how did I discover it? By having HR send me her file, and reading it over and over again.

I like to think I'm more moral than Sev, which admittedly doesn't take much. But equally, I don't have a spotless record, especially if you go back to my early years in Milan. Or last month with Mr Hathaway.

If she knew... Miss Meadows wouldn't tell me where she was if she didn't trust me. There's nothing to keep me hoping, not dots indicating an update on the screen as I watch the static background and re-read our exchange while Sev says unhelpful younger brother things, like, "We could put a tracker on her handbag."

But then it appears, popping up with no text. Just a map with a precise location in London.

"Good girl," I breathe, my chest relaxing like I've recovered from a heart attack.

Sev quirks an eyebrow and smirks. "Like that, is it?"

I'm on my feet. "I'm going out. You stay here."

"This is your house." Sev looks at me like I'm crazy.

"Don't trash it. You can drink yourself stupid, if you want." I shove my suit jacket on, but don't bother looking in a mirror, or putting on a tie. I stride down the long, white corridor at a pace that is only just not a run.

"Where are you going?" Sev keeps up with me.

"To a bar."

"Sounds fun. I'll come with you."

"No." But I don't do more than mutter, "Fuckwit" when he gets into the passenger side of the car. It's nice to not be totally on my own. I guess. Even if he isn't the person I really want to be with: Cassie.

5

CASSIE

This evening is a mistake.

The three shots I've downed while messaging Mr Blackwood have gone to my head and I'm still left with four more. I can't get rid of this man beside me, I can't catch the eye of my housemates, I'm rapidly losing faith with my plan to lose my V-card, and I've gained a boyfriend more fictional and perfect than any I've read in a book.

I fiddle with my phone, checking to see if Mr Blackwood has replied since I sent him my location, as he demanded.

Nothing.

I suppose he just wants to know where I am so he could tell the police my last movements if I'm murdered.

On the plus side, after stress-drinking three shots, I am down to just four, which surely I can manage to carry?

"So, your *boyfriend*." The man emphasises it as though he doesn't believe me, and leans in. "He's coming tonight, is he?"

I nod, hoick up my purse onto my shoulder, pull down

my dress—again—and try to pick up the shot glasses. "Probably. He's got a lot of work to do, though."

"Not here right now. Maybe he's too *high-powered* to come out with you on Friday night? That doesn't sound like a good boyfriend, leaving you all alone."

"He's the best." I attempt to sound confident as I awkwardly try to pick up the shot glasses without spilling brightly-coloured vodka everywhere. Third attempt I manage it. So long as no one jostles me, I'll be fine.

"I can help with that, if you like," the man says casually. He's persistent as a fly.

"No!" I yelp. "No, that's not needed." A miracle, that's what's needed.

And for once, luck is on my side, because cutting a line across the room are my housemates.

"Hey, Cassie." Julie sheds glitter from her dress as she moves and eyes the man who has been—I don't know what to call it. Chatting me up? Negging me? Talking to me? "What you got?"

"I've got shot—" I hold up my hands.

"Nice to meet you." Tamara reaches across me, practically shouldering me out of the way to shake the hand of the man, and so doing, nudges the precariously held shot glasses.

They spill all over me. Right down the front of my cream dress pours yellow, green, blue, and red vodka.

I look in disbelief.

Fuck. My. Life.

The colours mix together and are instantly yellow, brown-ish green, and purple-ish red. It's even on my shoes.

For a second, I close my eyes. Needles gently stab my eyelids. Worst night ever.

"Oh, you spilt your drink," Tamara says insincerely. "Bad luck. What took you so long, anyway?"

"She's been texting her boyfriend," the man says.

"You didn't tell me you had a boyfriend!" Julie says, mock scandalised. "Naughty!"

"Mm." Nodding, I dump the now-empty shot glasses onto the bar. I would try to indicate to Julie that I'm lying to keep this guy away because she and the other two left me alone and disappeared off to dance, but I think she'd enjoy outing and humiliating me.

"When did that happen?" Julie asks.

"Quite recently." I look around for some napkins or something to repair the damage to my dress. Or maybe just wipe my sticky hands on, but there's nothing. "You know, when I've not been home."

"I thought you were working. I'm sure Polly said your boss was making you work late."

"No." I turn to my tormentors, giving up on all dignity. Being covered in multi-coloured vodka does that. "Not weekends and evenings. Obviously." I laugh as though that's absurd, but it's not.

And now I told Mr Blackwood he's a bad boss, and I'm going to die of either how much I love him or a simple assassination for calling him a bad boss, we'll see which happens sooner.

"What's he like?" Julie asks in a gossipy, faux-friendly way that makes me want to barf.

"Italian." And I could bite my tongue off. "But his accent is subtle."

"Italian." Tamara draws out the word, and I can tell she doesn't believe me.

"He's tall." My hands are sticky, and my palms are sweating. I want out of here. "Bright blue eyes."

I am describing my boss. I tried, I really did, but he's the only man I want.

"Actually tall, or like, taller than you?" Julia's lip curls.

"Six-foot-three. Dark-brown hair. He's a bit older than me and has a high-powered job." Those first two things are facts, the third and fourth are massive understatements.

"Pics or it didn't happen." She winks and puts her hand on her hip.

"I don't have any photos of him." Wow, I am just as pathetic as I feel in my stained dress. "He doesn't like having his photo taken."

"He doesn't like having his photo taken." Polly and Tamara glance at each other and smirk.

I lower my gaze. I can't even lie to their faces. I swallow down my humiliation just as there are raised voices at the entrance to the bar. A group of well-dressed men have come in, and I spot him instantly, as though he's permanently highlighted in blue.

Mr Blackwood.

He's with another man who looks just like him—one of his brothers presumably—looking around the bar, searching. I still.

He's here.

And that's the moment he spots me.

"Is this him?" Julie looks Mr Blackwood up and down as though he's a tree she'd like to climb. Possessive jealousy curdles in my stomach along with the alcohol. Mr Blackwood is my crush. He's my grumpy boss, and I don't want *anyone else* having him. Or even looking at him.

Our gazes lock and without taking his eyes off me, he strides through the room, the crowd parting like he's a god.

He might as well be. He's tall, gorgeous, in absolute control. Everyone else melts away.

"Cass..." He seems to catch himself from saying my first name. "Miss Meadows." Mr Blackwood takes in my stained dress with a scowl.

"I spilt my drink," I explain, my voice very small, and show him my sticky hands as though that makes it clearer. I am a doof.

He gestures with one finger and the barman is there instantly. "Clean cloth, please. And a glass of water."

Within seconds, he has what he's requested, and I peek up at him from under my lashes, embarrassed as he takes one of my hands in his, then the other, and wipes them clean, expression impassive.

Discarding the cloth, he wraps my fingers around the glass of water and instructs me to drink.

Not having much choice, I gulp it down and Mr Blackwood removes his suit jacket. The man who was badgering me has gone, I realise, and so has Mr Blackwood's brother and at least one of the men with them. I wonder uneasily if those things are related.

Mr Blackwood plucks the glass from my hand as I finish it, and then wraps his jacket around my shoulders, impatiently indicating for me to put my arms in. Then he has me in it, the front buttoned, and the arms rolled up. It's ludicrously big on me, I'm dwarfed. It's longer than my dress.

Tugging at the lapels, my boss scowls at the low-cut neckline of my dress that his jacket does nothing to hide, then his gaze meets mine, and I melt. His eyes. My god, his blue eyes.

What is he doing here?

"I can't believe your boyfriend arrived, Cassie." Julia's interjection into this moment is about as welcome as presents from a pet cat. "We were beginning to think you'd made him up."

Mr Blackwood goes rigid and turns to her. "I'm not her boyfriend."

My cheeks heat. There was my thinking this evening had taken a turn for the better, and yeah nope. It's worse.

"Huh." Julie gives me a look like, *I knew you were lying.* "That's odd. Because she described someone exactly like you as her boyfriend."

Julie sweeps Mr Blackwood with a speculative gaze now she knows he's not mine, and I'm torn between bitch fighting her, and bursting into tears.

Mr Blackwood's gaze bounces between me—the mortified raspberry—and Julie, the smug blonde. There would be silence if it weren't for the noise of voice and the drumming of music.

I'm utterly humiliated. I might vomit.

"Didn't you say he was tall, with bright blue eyes? Brown hair," Julie says to me then turns to Mr Blackwood. "She said her *boyfriend* was rich, and handsome."

My chin droops, but like a rabbit caught in headlights, I'm unable to actually move. I should run. That's the mature thing to do right now having been caught out.

That or break into song. "*It wasn't me.*"

Except it was. I said all that, and all three of us in this conversation know full well I was thinking of my hot boss when I described my "boyfriend".

"She said that was where she'd been every evening this last month," Julie continues, getting right into her smug glee as I attempt to sink into the floor. "And that he had a hint of an Italian accent, which I think you do, isn't that right?"

Julie sidles right up to Mr Blackwood. "You have such a broad chest though." She reaches up and smooths across Mr Blackwood's undeniably broad chest. "She didn't say her boyfriend keeps in such good shape, and she would have mentioned it given you must work so hard at the gym..."

It's more difficult than it looks, sinking into the floor. I need tips on disappearing. I could take up magic, or just immigrate to the moon. Perhaps NASA would lob me into space like that dog.

Maybe an expedition to the bottom of the ocean. One-way ticket.

Mr Blackwood's hand strikes Julie's and rips it from his chest.

"I'm not her boyfriend," he states in a furious voice. "I'm her *fiancé*."

6

VITO

"You're engaged?" Cassie's friend's mouth drops open.

"I told you that I was serious about marriage, amore mio dolce," I continue, focusing on Cassie. "But I appreciate that without a ring you might not have understood."

I've called her that a million times in my head, and the affectionate expression slips out naturally. She looks so cute in my jacket, and seeing her wearing my clothes soothes all my protective instincts that went haywire when I saw her in that dress so small it could be a vest. Damn it, I want to be the only one who sees those beautiful legs.

"Engaged..." Drawls a familiar voice behind me. "This is news to me too, brother."

Sev.

Cassie looks between the two of us, and I grit my teeth. Why the hell didn't I murder my youngest brother anytime between five minutes ago and forty years ago? He's nothing but trouble.

"Lovely to meet you." He flashes Cassie a calculating smile.

"Come and dance with me." I snatch up her hand before she can say anything.

"Oh-okay," she stammers as I practically drag her away.

The possessive beast in me is wild with the need to have her alone.

"Sort the music. Something slow and classic," I order in an undertone as we pass one of my men.

In the knot of dancers on the wooden floor, Cassie stands paralysed, almost cowering. A scared little fawn.

I draw her to me, wrapping one arm around her waist and shifting her hand in mine until we're close-dancing. I ignore the style of the music and just dance to the off-beat. She looks up, her soft blue eyes meeting mine, expression confused even as she follows my lead perfectly. Like she's made for me.

Then her gaze flits to the side nervously. "They're all watching."

"Better give them something to see, then." I'm only too happy to, leaning down to murmur in her ear. "Fiancée."

"Oh god." She ducks her chin with embarrassment. "I didn't know you were a white knight," she whispers back. "Thank you."

"Not at all." If she only knew how black my soul is. And I'm a bad boss. The worst. Her accusation echoes in my head. I push it away. All that matters is that I'm here for her, and whatever she said, she hasn't refused my help.

She sneaks a look to the side, and it unsettles her rhythm, sending her left as I move right, and she cringes. "I can't dance old-fashioned ballroom style."

"Look at me." She obeys and I smile. "Follow my lead." I lift my arm to guide her into an underarm turn, which makes her splutter with laughter. I love to see her spark back.

"Like you did," she points out. "Playing along with my lie. Dancing with the girl covered in flavoured vodka."

"Is that what the scent is? Cherry? I love fruit salad." Actually, all I can smell is her vanilla scent, stronger now she's near me. I want to gobble her up.

That coaxes a smile from her, but it sours. "Lending the loser your jacket."

I guide her hand to my shoulder, hold her back tight, lean her into a low dip, and growl into her ear, "Don't talk about yourself that way."

And by the time she's upright again, she's flushed and when I take her hand and cover it with mine on my chest, she blinks like she's never seen me before. And perhaps she hasn't.

The thing about me being a bad boss has hit painfully close to the truth, and her saying I'm her boyfriend has unleashed something that I haven't allowed out in a long time. Maybe not since I was a kid in London with my triplet brothers.

"The jacket looks better on you than me," I add, and she presses her lips together, hiding a smile. She's so beautiful. I wish I knew how to tell her that.

"This isn't how you dance to this sort of music, you know." Then her eyes go wide as the music seamlessly fades into a slow song that you absolutely do dance like this to, and I lead her into another underarm turn, then another, until she's giggling despite herself.

Over her shoulder, I catch the eye of Tony as he backs away from the DJ booth, pocketing his wallet. We exchange nods before I look back down at Cassie.

"Do people always do what you want them to?" she asks.

I smile wryly, and think of Sev, Rafe, and her. She

doesn't always do what I want, or we wouldn't be *pretending* that we were engaged. "I wish they did."

"But you can magically change the tune to suit you?" She says it like it's a puzzle, but lets me lead her, moving with me. And for the first time in a long, long time, I'm at peace.

This is where she belongs: in my arms, our bodies almost touching.

"This sort of dancing makes it easier to talk. And we needed to, don't you think?" I don't understand why my power, or what I decide we dance to, is a big deal. There are actually important things, like how can I ensure she's more than a one-night fiancée?

"Ah. Yeah." She ducks her head and mutters, "Sorry."

"Do you have a boyfriend?" I hold my breath.

"No," she whispers, gaze sliding away.

The pure jealousy eases a bit and air expands my lungs again.

"Why did you make one up?" I don't quite ask why she described him as being precisely like me, but we'll get to that.

"There was a man bothering me," she says, and my hand tightens on her waist.

"That won't be a problem again," I swear. Mainly because I suspect he's already dead. Sev hasn't got much patience, and I asked him to deal with the man who was standing too close to Cassie. But even if Sev was uncharacteristically merciful, he made my girl uncomfortable and that's a death wish. Doesn't matter that he didn't know she's mine.

Well, alright. He might survive with a maiming, I reflect as Cassie and I move together, completely in sync. He gave me the perfect excuse to be close to the woman I love.

"Okay. So how long have I been your boyfriend?"

"A month," she admits miserably, focusing on my top button.

I can't help but smile. A month. All the time I've known her. I can live with that. "And I guess we've been engaged since yesterday."

I need to get her a ring. One with a big diamond that says what I can't put into words: I want this to be real, whatever the cost.

"You don't have to do this. I might just go home. This isn't my scene really."

I ignore the comment about not being her fake fiancé, because there's no way in hell I'm giving that up now. I am as committed to our lie as a five-year-old saying they haven't eaten chocolate cake when they have chocolate smeared across their cheeks.

"Why are you here then?" We continue dancing and it's so obviously a prelude to how well she'll fit me when I make love to her, my cock is getting chubby.

"I wanted to..." She catches her lower lip in her teeth. "Maybe try and meet someone."

"Anyone caught your eye?" My tone is light, but I hope she says no for everyone's sake.

She shakes her head and my chest eases. I am a bastardo in truth, because I'm glad she won't be happy with another man, at least for now. I can't have her because she's too young and sweet, but I can indulge in our fake engagement.

"And now you're engaged," I point out.

Her smile is rueful. "That was really kind of you. But why are you even here?"

It's my turn to slip my gaze away, and sweep her into a spin to hide while I think. I consider lying, but settle for a half-truth.

"Because you messaged me on your Friday night off, and it sounded like you needed help."

I leave out the part about missing her, wishing for any excuse to see her, and wanting her in my life for more than work. I don't say that I love her with the whole of my sorry excuse for a soul.

"I'm sorry I interrupted your evening. And your brother's."

I snort. "Sev doesn't deserve your sympathy. He's enjoying himself."

We both glance across to the bar where my brother has his phone out and is pointedly ignoring Cassie's friends, who are trying to get his attention.

"I almost wish I'd seen Julie's face when you said you were my fiancé. I was too shocked to enjoy it fully."

"It was quite a moment." That I also missed, because I only have eyes for Cassie. "Now we have our story straight, do you want to fully enjoy proving her wrong?"

The way she bites her lip and gets this naughty little smile tells me all I need to know. She'd be such a perfect mafia boss' wife, with that vengeful streak. Moreover, I'm increasingly aroused by dancing with a girl half my age, so perhaps some acting to allow her to revel in being right, rather than tempting me, would be a good idea. I haven't forgotten about her stained dress under my jacket, either.

"Gloating allowed," I tell her, and I keep my hand on her waist, guiding her back to the bar.

"Wait, what should I call you?" she hisses as we get near.

Husband. "Vito."

Cassie's so-called friends turn curious and slightly fearful stares at us as soon as we're within range. I ignore them.

"On your phone again, Sev?" I greet my brother. "I thought you didn't approve."

"Vaffanculo," he says ironically, flicking the screen blank and shoving it into his pocket.

"Is that Italian? What does that mean?" Cassie asks.

"It's a brotherly expression of love," I say dryly.

"The closest translation is 'go fuck yourself,'" Sev tells her.

Cassie's friends greet her at a pitch thankfully not audible because I'm too old and not a dog.

Joking, sadly it is. I internally debate whether it would be unacceptable to kill them, and decide that unfortunately, it's Cassie's decision, not mine. I'll offer to get rid of them as a wedding present.

"So how long have you two been together?" One of her friends asks.

"I uh." Cassie looks terrified. "About... I mean..."

"A month." My tone is firm.

"And where did you meet?" Sev looks as innocent as the choir girl he lost his virginity to many years ago. He knows something is up, and is tormenting me.

Cassie looks up at me in panic.

We really should have discussed this instead of flirting, and I clench my jaw. "Looking for dating tips, Sev?"

"I'm just interested in my big brother's life." He's practically polishing his halo. "You've never had any woman you talked about while you were in Milan. Then, the minute you're back in London, you're engaged."

"It is very odd you've never mentioned your boyfriend before," Cassie's friend adds. That bitch looks far too happy that Cassie is shrinking down.

Fine. They want evidence? That suits me.

"They don't believe us, amore mio dolce," I murmur. "It's time for show, not tell."

I slip my arm around Cassie's waist and pull her to me. My instinct is to pause and look into her eyes before I lower my head.

I don't. If we were engaged, this wouldn't be our first kiss. I would kiss Cassie often, thoroughly, and until her lower leg kicked up like in a black-and-white movie. I'd kiss her until her lips were plump and red, and then I'd kiss her everywhere else.

But for now, one kiss.

I'll take the kiss I'm surely owed.

After all, Cassie Meadows is my fiancée.

7

CASSIE

The moment Vito's lips touch mine, all my bones go to jelly. I never realised a kiss would be like this, or I'd have tried it earlier. His mouth is warm and firm, and sending little zings in all directions. Up into my overwhelmed mind, and down to my fluttery belly. And beyond. Between my legs a coil slowly, slowly tightens.

He holds my neck, caressing it gently and probably holding me up, too, because I've melted into him. His tongue plunders my mouth, stroking, invading. It's carnal and hot and I hang onto him, trying to look like I'm doing something I've done a million times as my world turns inside out from one fake kiss.

Dancing with Mr Blackwood was magic.

Kissing him is a portal to another realm. I've never had a vivid imagination, I did accounting, after all. Boring. But I've read spicy books and assumed that the women who wrote them had extraordinary minds, because I hadn't noticed frissons of excitement from glances with men. And now I have to admit, they aren't making it up. Being kissed by Vito Blackwood, my gorgeous, powerful boss, really is that good.

And he's kissing me in front of my housemates who laugh at me, making me feel desirable and beautiful and not just included, but important.

The centre of his world.

He's an outstanding actor, I vaguely think as he holds my head to tilt it as his mouth slides over mine. He's a surprise. A classy and dominant dancer, making it feel effortless with two-left-feet me, and after all these days being surly, a charming if brusque, fake boyfriend.

"Alright, you made your point," Mr Blackwood says, and I stiffen out of instinct to not upset the man I want to impress so much. It takes my brain a moment to recognise his accent is wrong. Too much Britain, not enough Italy. It's not my Mr Blackwood, but the *other* Mr Blackwood. My Mr Blackwood is still kissing me, one hand clasped on my waist and the other in my hair.

Oh no.

My Mr Blackwood? I'm a goner. This will break me. I cannot think of my boss as being *mine*.

He draws back and gives me a long, slow smile that turns my knickers to liquid butter.

"Let's go somewhere more private," he says in a voice that's pure sex. It sounds like he really wants to take me back to his house and fuck me until I can't walk.

"Yes," I reply breathlessly.

"Don't you have a bar bill to settle?" Julie snips, and through the fog of arousal Vito—it's so deliciously forbidden to think of my boss as Vito—I recognise she's jealous. Of *me*.

The sensation is as foreign as it is delicious.

"I'll cover it," Mr Blackwood says smoothly.

"No, no." I'll pay for my own mistakes, and I'm proud of

making a good salary. I approach the bar, and the barman comes over immediately. Nothing like the power of being with a mafia boss.

Dragging my purse off my shoulder and rifling through it, I try to find the credit card I know is there somewhere. I shove aside a clean pair of knickers and a stick of lip salve. I can feel Mr Blackwood watching me intently and my neck prickles with heat and embarrassment and something else that's not unlike pleasure in their weirdest way.

Then—ah!—I spy the glint of plastic. "There it is!" I burrow deeper into my purse and carefully keep the knickers stuffed down as I pull out the card.

I wave it triumphantly at the barman who has wandered off to serve someone else while I had my little purse drama.

"You dropped something," Mr Blackwood says.

"I found..." But the words die in my throat as Mr Blackwood picks up one of the condoms I bought earlier between two fingers and examines it with an expression of distaste.

"What's this?" His voice is dangerously soft.

"I don't know," I squeak, the card suddenly tight in my hand. My emotional support bank card. Proof that I am an adult with a bank account and a job—currently—and sensible things like an overdraft I pay off every month and good financial sense as well as a very dusty V-card.

Because oh god. This is so bad.

The wrapper is bright pink, with a pair of red lips on it. It proudly proclaims that it is strawberry flavoured. Extra strong. Ribbed for her pleasure.

And *glow in the dark*.

Pink. And glow in the dark.

What was I *thinking*?

Obviously, not that my boss would ever see it. I bought

one of every type of condom from the vending machine in the toilets. With all that has happened, I totally forgot about my mission to get laid.

I'm more likely to get knocked out from sheer bad luck than smuggle the sausage in the pink canal.

"You don't know." Mr Blackwood sounds unconvinced, as he has every right to be.

Who do I think I'm kidding? Breathe, Cassie, breathe. You can do this. You are an actual adult.

Behind me, my housemates titter.

"A condom."

"I can see that," he says with smoothly exaggerated patience. "Why do you have it in your purse for a night out with the girls, when you *have a fiancé?*"

There are plenty of good reasonable answers I could give. Things like, *you're my fake fiancé.* And, *it's none of your business since you are my boss, and this is Friday night when most normal people are relaxing, drinking alcopops, dancing, and having casual sex.*

Admittedly, I am not like most people, because I have spent the last four Friday nights being grilled by my hot boss about sexy, sexy things like Gantt charts.

Mr Blackwood drops the strawberry condom, gritting his teeth so hard I can almost feel the vibrations of it above the pulse of the bar's music.

He drags his gaze over the banana-flavoured one, yellow and glow-in-the-dark, obviously.

"You were going to use these, tonight?" His brows are lowered, his blue eyes glittering.

"No! Of course not!"

"But you bought them." He's thunder. "You were going to use them. Three of them."

I don't know why he's acting like he's really my fiancé,

and he's possessive of me, but my brain is mush. There's no pretending they were for him. Mr Blackwood is not the sort of man who would wear a purple condom. Or glow-in-the-dark pink.

"For balloon animals?"

"Miss Meadows," he growls.

"Water bombs."

Next to Vito, his brother snorts with laughter and I die internally.

"Are you a five-year-old, Miss Meadows?" Mr Blackwood asks severely.

"Cut price gloves." I'm babbling. I've lost the plot. All sense of what's appropriate or not has gone right out the window. After all, I was the one who told my housemates that someone exactly like my boss in every detail was my boyfriend.

"Do I not pay you enough?" There's a sinister edge to the words.

"Oh, he is her boss!" exclaims Tamara, and I really don't know how I'm going to explain any of this to anyone. I might just move to Outer Mongolia instead.

"Budget chewing gum." I press my lips together to prevent myself from saying anything more.

I bet yak farming is really fun. Compared to my hot boss discovering my impulse-buy condoms.

"Cassie."

Simultaneously, I melt and combust. The way he says my name in that gruff voice gives me the crazed impulse to snuggle into him and lick his neck where his dark stubble gives way to smooth skin.

It's a physical impossibility—not least because he's too tall for me to do that—but rather like my interest in sex suddenly bloomed when I met my boss, it's a force of nature. My libido is one of those plants that blooms only once for one day in like a hundred years and the rest of the time is a plain green thing with nothing interesting at all about it. In fact, don't those plants die after they bloom for that single day?

Never mind, never mind. That hardly matters, because I will already be deceased from sheer embarrassment. My cheeks are a heating element on an old-fashioned cooker, glowing neon red. You could fry eggs on my face.

Mr Blackwood takes a deep breath.

"Amore mio dolce. It was thoughtful of you to buy condoms, but you must believe me this time. There's no need for contraception, because *I want* to get you pregnant."

My jaw falls open. It's an even more public claim than the kiss. From the corner of my eye, I see that the smirks are wiped from Julie, Tamara, and Polly's faces and replaced with an expression that with a jolt I realise is jealousy.

I just watch in shock as Mr Blackwood shakes his head fondly at me, makes some wordless communication with the barman who presumably knows a Blackwood pays his debts, then grabs my purse, and leaving the condoms strewn on the bar, takes my hand in his, and tugs me to his side.

He presses a kiss to my forehead and then announces to the room in general, "I'm taking *my fiancée* home."

8

VITO

The tension between us is a steel wire as we ride to my house. Dark shrouds the back of the car, with flickering yellow from the streetlights.

Now we're alone, I'm kicking myself, because there's no reason to fake, is there? I let go of her hand as we got into the car, and the chasm of thick black and silence between us makes it impossible to reach across and touch her again. To do so would be saying I deserve her, and I don't.

I've returned to being her boss.

I'm old enough to be her father, I remind myself.

"I thought you were taking me home." The whites of her eyes glint when we stop outside my London city residence and one of my men opens the door for her.

"We're celebrating our engagement, aren't we? Mustn't have your friends thinking I'm not serious. I assumed you'd want to stay. Just tonight." That sounds reasonable. Not at all like I'm obsessed with getting her into my house like I'm Beast stealing Beauty.

"Just for show, then?" she checks. "So my housemates don't realise because I've gone straight home."

A sound that could be agreement or denial comes from my throat as I lead her into the house. I tell myself I take her to my room because I know for sure that there are towels in the bathroom and clean sheets, and she's tired and shouldn't have to wait. I'm pretty sure the housekeeper keeps a dozen guest rooms pristine at all times, but I want her in my space. I'll enjoy torturing myself with the image of the one time she was in my house.

"I thought you'd want to clean up," I say as she looks around my bedroom. By sheer willpower I don't add anything about helping her out of her wet clothes, or being happy to help her get dirty again. But I repeat the cheesy lines in my head.

I point out the ensuite. "There's a shower, or bath. Just take whatever you need. Help yourself to anything from the wardrobe to sleep in."

She snuggles into my suit jacket, pulling it tighter around her as though I might try to take it away. No chance. What's mine is hers. Peeking up at me from beneath her lashes, she says, "Where will you be?"

"Downstairs in the lounge." I'm too wired to sleep. "Good night."

Then I practically run from the room. There's only so much temptation a man can resist.

It takes a while to hear the report from the men I had with me tonight. Sev, it turns out, only gave the man who was harassing Cassie at the bar a scare, and ripped bits off him that will grow back. I instruct Tony to keep an eye on him and ensure if he pushes unwanted attention on a woman again, that will be the last time.

I feel very superior for not actually having him murdered. Perhaps I should join the London Mafia oo-but-we-don't-kill-people-unless-we-have-to Syndicate, after all.

Eventually, I collapse onto a sofa in the lounge, the late summer night still not fully dark outside and I field a few obnoxious texts from Sev, and curious ones from my other triplet, Rafe, who is with his wife. She was his assistant, and now they have a baby on the way. Fucker. I'm not jealous of his happiness. Except, I am.

A beer sits on the table next to me, untouched, as I sit back and think about Cassie this evening. Of her sweet lips and her adorable laugh. She's the only one I want.

There's a little bird tap at the door, and a gorgeous brown-blonde head peeks around the frame. "Hello."

She's barefoot as she slips into the room, and wearing nothing but my pale blue shirt. My heart sticks in my throat. Like the suit jacket, seeing her in my clothes again is just as powerful as last time. Her legs are fabulous, and I can't help but stare. Then I drag my gaze to her face and find she's got hope in her eyes.

I don't understand.

She tugs on the hem of the shirt. "Is this okay?"

My throat is drier than a houseplant without my staff.

"It's longer than the dress I was wearing." She smiles ruefully.

"Why are you down here, amore mio dolce?"

She presses her lips together and approaches, before curling onto the sofa next to me. "I was thinking in the shower."

I watch her, even as my pulse ticks up along with the way my shirt has tugged up to reveal more of her biteable thigh.

"That's the place where the best ideas happen."

"Yes!" Her face lights. "That's where I had this idea."

"What was that?" I'm a bit afraid of what my tipsy girl might have thought of.

"You helped me once this evening, by pretending to be my fiancé." She takes a deep breath. "Would you help me with something else?"

"If I can," I reply cautiously.

"I wanted to get rid of my V-card this evening." She says it in a rush.

And that's when my heart stops. Because this gorgeous woman who has been in my fantasies since we met—the image I've jerked my cock to, the name on my lips as I've come, my obsession—is untouched?

"Just as a favour," she adds. "Purely practical, like pretending to be my fiancé. You were really good at that, and I wondered if you'd be kind and help me with this too."

"You're a virgin?" I croak.

She blushes and closes her eyes. "Mmm."

"That's..." So hot that she'd be mine alone. I'd be the first one to breach my lovely girl. "Not possible tonight." It's taking all my strength to not say that I would be honoured to help her with this. That I will do it right now, and she'll come on my cock over and over again.

"Vito..." She puts on an ingratiating voice and opens those pretty pale eyes to entreat me. "Will you—"

"No." Absolutely not. If I take her virginity, I'll never let her go. I don't think I'd allow her out of my sight. She deserves better. At the very least, she should make the decision when she's got a clear head.

"Please. Please, pretty-please, fiancé." She crawls over me and my arms come up without my volition. They settle on her waist. It's perfectly nipped in, her hips flaring out and my mouth waters as I regard the swell of her tits. My shirt has ridden up, and a scrap of white is visible between her legs. Her knickers. I bite back a groan. She was made for my hands and my cock responds with the inevitability of being near her.

"Cassie..." I can't help but tighten my grip. She's so incredibly sweet.

"Mr Blackwood." Her eyes sparkle like sunshine on a lake.

"Vito." If I'll be damned for this night, I will have my name on her lips this once.

"Vito," she repeats, and it's everything. I could listen to her on a loop forever. I groan. How am I ever going to return to calling her Miss Meadows and keeping my distance?

"We can't. You're drunk." Who am I trying to convince? No one. It's a fact. She wouldn't be doing this if she was thinking straight.

"I'm not. I'm very sober." She sounds so uninhibited—not drunk but definitely tipsy—that I laugh, and she looks at me as though *I'm* sunshine, and that breaks me.

"Amore mio dolce," I breathe.

"You will?" She makes a little purring noise and pushes closer, wrapping her arms around me and wriggling her hips, trying to get friction on her needy clit.

"No."

She stills, and her face falls, the spark gone from her and the sexy confidence hissing out like a punctured balloon.

I allow myself the pleasure of combing my fingers into her hair. It's incredibly soft. I tilt her head up to look at me again. "But I will let you use my fingers to make yourself come."

That's an acceptable compromise, isn't it?

The way she perks up says, yes. Yes, this is the right thing.

"I will if you tell me what to do," she whispers, as though this is a secret between the two of us, and if she speaks too loudly, she'll break the spell, or someone else will hear.

"Take off your knickers," I tell her. "And sit on my lap."

She wriggles off, giving me a delicious view of the swell of her soft tits as she pushes her white cotton underwear down her thighs. So. Perfect.

"Can I touch you too?" she asks as she toys with the buttons of my shirt that she's wearing.

"No." That's a temptation too far. Her small hand trying to clasp my length? Too much, and I can't be sure I wouldn't take more than I ought. But my curt response makes her hesitate, and no. None of that. So I just tell her the truth. "I'm yours to do with as you wish. But let me spoil you first."

"Except take my virginity." Her pout is so kissable.

"Except that." Though I want it. I really, really do. But more than I crave her tight, wet, hot little pussy over my cock, I need her to never regret anything we do. If we have sex, it'll be a forever promise with a ring and making a baby. "I will make you come so hard you'll feel the echo in a week."

She makes a needy little sound.

"Now." I crook my finger. "Come here and kiss me." That glimpse I had of her pussy lips glistened, and I'm keen to discover if she's as eager for this as she seems.

I slide my palm down her thigh as she settles on my lap again. Between us, my cock is a steel rod, thick and heavy.

She's tentative as she leans in. Our lips touch.

It's fire. I nibble and suck and she presses her palms to my chest, shifting closer as our mouths engage in a leisurely dance. It's like we've done this thousands of times before, so natural. The crackling chemistry between us is undeniable.

This time as I sink my hand into her hair, she arches as I

tug and reveals her neck. I kiss down it, making her shudder. I indulge in that, with little bites that make her gasp, and will leave marks.

Then, taking her hand, I rub my thumb over her small palm and then twist my hand so her fingers cover mine, partly at least. She blinks as I lower our hands together to rest lightly on her thigh.

"Show me how wet you are."

She makes a needy sound and squirms and pushes my hand down, until my fingertips brush her mons.

"Brave girl." And I see she glows with my praise before she kisses me again and presses my fingers into her slit. Slick, warm arousal drips onto my knuckles.

"Absolutely soaked," I observe. "That's so good. Now show me where you need me to touch you, Cassie."

"Here," she whispers back. "Stroke me. Make me come. Please, Mr Blackwood."

"Vito," I remind her.

"Vito." Pressing her mouth to mine, she kisses me desperately as I explore her folds with infinitesimal slowness. "I've never done this before. Help me."

"You've never made yourself come?" I ask in disbelief.

She shakes her head, and I gather her closer to me, kissing her with all the pent-up desire of the last month.

"I never wanted to until..." That statement is left hanging.

"Innocent girl. Amore mio dolce." I whisper other romantic and filthy words in Italian. Around kisses and in a language she doesn't understand, I tell her how hot and perfect her little pussy is, and that I didn't think I could love her any more, but her being this innocent fills my heart with pride and engorges my cock beyond what I thought possible.

All the while, I caress the bare nape of her neck and slip my fingertips over her slit, circling and gradually approaching the little untouched nub.

As my finger brushes her clit she gasps, I smirk. "That's right. I'm going to make you fly."

She grasps my lapels, and while I rub over her clit, she holds herself to me.

"That's a good girl." And because she squirms and pants more, I add. "You're being such a good girl for me."

"Vito." Cassie is losing it, slumping against me and open-mouth kissing my neck.

"Reach for it. Feel that pressure building inside you? Drag it towards you."

She's keening now as her climax approaches.

"You're my good girl." I increase the pace of the thrusts of my fingers inside her, rubbing that sensitive inside wall hard, and feeling how she shudders in my arms.

She screams, convulsing on my fingers.

"So beautiful." I hold her to me as she breaks, pulsing on my fingers again and again, before eventually slumping as her climax drops off. "This is what you wanted when you wore that tease of a dress, wasn't it?"

Her sigh is music. Exhausted, sated.

I shift her and stand, bringing her with me, and she only lets out a little squeak before nestling into me. I carry her upstairs, and tuck her into my bed, allowing myself the indulgence of kissing her forehead. Then I wrench myself away, and fall back into a chair. To keep watch over her until morning.

9

CASSIE

It's dark when I wake, but my mind is full of last night.

All of it. Every embarrassing mistake is technicolour in my poor brain. I wish I had amnesia. In fact, I am not ruling that out as a strategy. Because not only am I in my boss' bed wearing nothing but his shirt, I am not sure where he is. Tentatively, I feel around me. Nothing. I open my eyes, and they gradually adjust to the low light. I pick out shapes in grey against the black.

I asked my boss to take my virginity.

And he said, *no*.

Oh god. How am I ever going to face him again? I've never had a morning after the night before, but I feel confident this level of embarrassment could be the end of me. He made me orgasm, sure, but he's not in bed with me, is he?

Crap.

That lie about him being my boyfriend is enough to make me crease like a soda can in absolute cringe. And my kind boss went along with it. And the condoms. Strawberry flavour ribbed condoms.

I press my head into the pillow.

I'm going to go to a hypnotist and have them remove these memories. Admittedly, that would get rid of the magical part when Vito made me come, but... Okay, instead could I learn hypnotism and make my boss forget?

Ughhh...

Sitting gingerly up, I look around the room. It takes me a second to see Mr Blackwood, sprawled in a chair. He has his long legs stretched out, casually crossed at the ankle, one hand on his knee and the other draped over the chair arm, and his head thrown back. His eyes are closed and his long dark lashes fan onto his cheeks and he's breathing deep and even. Every line of him is like a sleeping panther.

I'll let fate decide. If I can leave without him waking, I will. If he opens his eyes, I'll stay and face the most awkward conversation since Noah had to deal with the gay King Penguins boarding his arc.

In the darkness, I creep to where I left my dress, bra, purse, and shoes. I flush when I think of my white cotton knickers discarded somewhere downstairs.

It's a physical ache to unbutton Vito's shirt and push it from my shoulders. It smells like him: citrus and sandalwood. I take a long sniff before I hang it next to his jacket.

My dress is still a bit sticky and artificial smelling compared to the delicate, sophisticated scent of Vito's shirt. Instantly I'm less comfortable.

Gah. *Welcome to the rest of your life, Cassie.* Nothing will ever be as good as Vito's hands on me.

I look at my sleeping boss, and even in the dark, he's as beautiful as ever.

My feet take me to his side, to watch him like the psycho I am.

"'Bye," I breathe, and allow myself the indulgence of touching my lips to his cheek in the ghost of a kiss.

I'm almost disappointed he doesn't wake. But this is the right thing. Admittedly, also the cowardly thing, but trying the patience of mafia bosses is not something people who want to live do.

It takes me a couple of wrong turns through his enormous house, but eventually I make it downstairs into the hallway. Has my heart always been this loud? The sounds of the city are very faint, and my footsteps echo as I walk to the front door where we entered.

It's only as I try the handle that I realise my stupid error. This is the house of a mafia boss. Of course, the door is locked.

But as I glance across at the window and consider climbing out of it, there's a whirr and snick, and as though this is a fairy castle keen to eject its unwelcome guest, the door swings open.

I blink. How...?

Must be on a motion sensor of some kind, and anyone inside is allowed out. Maybe a fire safety thing?

I step into the cool, fragrant night air, and drag it into my lungs in a shaky gasp. I've left. I don't have to face my boss' kind brush-off in the morning, or do my first walk of shame in the daylight.

Pulling out my phone, I order an Uber as I walk to the front gate—also open. I don't even have to wait, as there's one available just around the corner and a sleek black SUV pulls up at the curb almost as soon as I've pressed the button.

The driver is an older woman with a polite smile, but even so, I feel worse and worse as the distance increases between Vito and me. Guilt and regret curdle in my stomach. I'm not even sure about what. Last night? Or leaving like a little thief?

But this is the right thing to do. I'm saving both Mr Blackwood and me a lot of discomfort in the morning.

I keep telling myself that, all the way home, and in bed when I can't sleep.

I'm brave. I can do this.

Or rather, I am fuelled by an obscene number of tubs of ice cream, some tears, and pecking out a resignation letter, an apology, a love letter, a horny confession, and finally another resignation letter.

The weekend was exceptionally long and miserable.

Vito didn't message. He didn't call.

I should have stayed for the humiliation of him being awake in the morning, because between soggy tissues and ill-fated writings where I said all the things I didn't know I felt, I realised I've fallen in love with my boss.

This weekend he didn't make any demands of work I should do, and I missed that. I need his attention more than orgasms, but I'm also strong enough to be honest: I made a fool of myself on Friday night, and there isn't any option but to move on, tend my broken heart so he doesn't realise I ever gave it to him.

Because however kind he is, he's my boss, a billionaire, and cared for me in a fatherly way last night. I think.

The signed resignation letter is tucked into my handbag as I enter work on Monday morning. Mr Blackwood's door is closed, and his secretary isn't in yet, and I tell myself this is fine. Vito probably won't be in for hours, and I have time to compose myself.

My office phone rings before I've sat down, and my pulse spikes. It's still early. There's only one person who calls outside of office hours.

"Hello." My voice quivers as I answer, and my arm isn't steady holding the receiver.

"Come to my office, Miss Meadows."

My throat goes dry, and I fail comprehensively to say anything.

"Now." Then he puts the phone down before my powers of speech return.

Snatching up my bag, I hurry to Mr Blackwood's door.

Oh god I am not ready for this.

There are prickles behind my eyes as I knock. I don't even understand Mr Blackwood's answer—it's just his customary bark—but I walk in with as much dignity as I can muster, and pin a smile on my face.

"Good morning, Mr Blackwood." My smile falters as I take him in. He looks tired, and all of his forty years. His usual pristine blue shirt is rumpled, and despite it being first thing in the morning he's not wearing a tie, or a jacket. There are dark circles under his eyes as though he slept about as much as I did this weekend, and he's scowling. The personal raincloud is back, hovering six inches above his head.

He's beautiful.

Seeing Vito again after thinking of him all weekend turns my brain into a bowl of soggy breakfast cereal, but the milk in this analogy is hormones, and cereal is longing. That makes no sense, but I am not logical. It's all I can do to not throw myself onto my boss' desk and beg him incoherently to call me his good girl again.

"Close the door, Miss Meadows," he says, low and deep.

The snick of the catch is loud in the otherwise silent

room. We're the only people on this floor, probably in the whole building. My shoes tap as I walk over to his desk with more confidence than I feel, my heart trying to vibrate out of my chest.

"What's this?" he asks as I place the letter on his desk.

I press my lips together and link my fingers in a death grip behind my back.

He reaches one big, dark hand across the shiny wood and pulls the single sheet towards him and all I can do is remember how that hand felt on me as he bows his head to read. How he clasped me to him, and played my body as though it was an instrument tuned perfectly to him. How he made me feel special and wanted and whispered in Italian as I broke apart from his touch.

A sob rises in my throat as his brows lower further and further. I've ruined everything with my ridiculous lie about him being my boyfriend. I could have just adored him from my office next door if I hadn't been so stupid.

He tosses the resignation letter away and it floats to the floor, catching under my toes.

Raising his eye line, he shakes his head. His blue eyes are hard as glass. "No. I'm not accepting your resignation."

"But—"

"I'll make you co-CEO."

I gape like a fish.

He shrugs one careless shoulder at my unspoken question. "Name your price for staying and working with me. Whatever you want, I'll make it happen. But you are not leaving."

Will my mouth ever close again? Doubtful. I'm so shocked I am full meme territory. This isn't going how I thought it would.

He leans forward, bracing his hands on the desk. "Why

did you describe me when you talked about your boyfriend?"

Because I've been thinking about you since we met. Because there's something about you that compels me. Because I think I love you, and on Friday night when you were so kind to me I think I fell...

Oh crap. I love him. I really, really love him.

I cannot say that.

"Why did you go along with it?" I whisper miserably. I still don't understand that. He's always cross with me. What made him suddenly change? Why did he have to be so good that my respect and physical attraction deepened into love?

He laughs cynically. "Ah, si."

Standing, he paces back and forth, and I watch, my heart in my throat. I don't know why.

He stops as abruptly as he began, and turns those violently blue eyes on me.

"I went along with it because I love you."

What? My chin jerks up.

"I said you were my fiancée because I want that more than anything else in the world," he continues matter of factly. "Except perhaps, for you to be my wife."

I'm struck dumb. Am I hallucinating?

"I'd do anything for you. I can't resist you."

"That's not possible," I say faintly.

He raises one, familiarly wry, eyebrow. "I assure you it is, amore mio dolce."

"But you're always so critical of me."

"What?" He steps back as though I've struck him. "When?"

Heat flushes up my neck. I'm an idiot. "Nothing."

"*When?*" he repeats more firmly.

"You criticise my posture," I mutter.

He creases his face in confusion. "I tell you to sit up straight because I don't want you to get back ache."

"You chastise me for snacking at my desk."

"You need to take breaks." He takes a step towards me, eyes softening. "You deserve to have a proper break."

"*Do you really need another mint, Miss Meadows,*" I mimic, and he shakes his head.

"Sugar between meals is bad for your teeth."

He has a point on that. I am a sugar addict. "And the sandwiches you objected to?"

"That is not food." Vito's expression is affronted. "I lived in Italy for twenty years. If you want bread, it should be of excellent quality. The sort of food to give you a long, wonderful, healthy life. Not cheap packaged sandwiches."

Have I misinterpreted everything about this situation?

"You told me off for fidgeting."

"Because I wanted you to be taken seriously by the rest of the team, as you deserve to be, and it made you appear nervous." His voice has gentled too, and he's standing right in front of me now.

I sway towards him, drawn in by his magnetic pull.

"Everything I said, I said out of love. Because I adore you, and I want you to be healthy and happy until at least a hundred so the world can have the blessing of you in it. And me. I want you in my life forever, and the thought of you having a bad back is unbearable to me. What else have I growled at you about, amore mio dolce?" His mouth twitches with a tug of amusement.

"You snapped at me for working late when it was *you* who insisted I redo all the numbers and so I had to stay late," I add. Final damning evidence.

I didn't mind the late night with him, but did he really have to be mean about it?

The laughter drops from his face, and he looks down at me with something like regret.

"Forgive me." He reaches out and brushes his knuckles over my cheek then rests there, blunt fingers on my jaw, stroking his thumb on my face. "I needed to see you. I craved being with you. I was out of my mind, and the only way I could think of for us to spend time together was to give you more work. But I also knew that you had to go home, and rest, and not be with me because you're my employee and I'm a grizzled kingpin old enough to be your father. I was trying to care for you the way you deserve."

Oh my heart. Is he going to continue saying things like this? I feel like my life has just been upgraded to First Class where I expected Economy.

"I don't care about your age. In fact, I..." Am I really going to confess that his grey hair and air of authority turn me on?

"Continue," he murmurs, sliding his other hand over my hip as he pushes his fingers into my hair to hold my head still.

"I like it," I admit. "I like that you're older and experienced. And you're my boss."

"Does it make you hot to have your older boss wrapped around your little finger?" He pulls me to him and the hardness of his erection presses into my belly, making excitement spiral through me. "I like that too, but if you'd prefer, you can be my barefoot, pregnant wife."

"Vito..." I breathe, and reach for him, looping my wrists at the back of his neck and standing on tiptoe.

"Now tell me, Miss Meadows." His voice drops to a hoarse whisper, and he leans down so our mouths are almost touching. "Tell me why you described me when you talked about your boyfriend."

"Because I wanted it to be true," I whisper, gazing into his blue eyes that are sparkling sapphires.

I only get a glimpse of his smile before he gathers me to him, his lips find mine, and he's kissing me.

And all my fears dissolve with the strength of how he holds me, and how right he feels. His grip tightens in my hair, shooting pinpricks of pain into my scalp that far from hurting, enhance the pleasure of his mouth.

Vito's passion matches my own. I try to climb him like the big dark cloud leading to heaven that he is. His kiss is bruising, powerful, and yet also sweet, even as he pulls me closer and closer, as though trying to meld us together.

"Mine. Cassie, I need you." He lifts me off my feet and carries me easily backwards until my bottom hits his solid desk. "You're mine, and I must have you. It's already been too long."

He pushes my cardigan off my shoulders as he kisses my neck, sending delicious shivers down my back.

"Bella. I've been dreaming of this, Cassie."

I'm so drunk on him that I don't protest as he tosses my purse aside and removes my clothes piece by piece, exploring with his hands and murmuring Italian words that sound like praise and appreciation as he presses his mouth to every revealed patch of skin. Nope, I revel in it. I arch and squirm and when he gets to my bra, I'm not even embarrassed by how large they are because he groans and cups both my breasts. And with his big hands on them, they don't look too big, they look just right. Then I look on, entranced, as he lowers his head and sucks one nipple into his mouth. The flare of pleasure pulls a cry from me, and he responds with a purr of delight.

He runs his hands down my sides until he gets to my trousers, which he undoes with indecent haste. And I help him. I don't point out that we're in his office, with the sun rising over London and the enormous windows letting in creamy morning light and that other staff could arrive, knock on the door, and enter at any moment. I just give in to whatever my boss wants, and apparently that's to undress and greedily touch every part of me.

I don't even care when after he slides my knickers off, I'm totally naked and he's still fully dressed, his only bare skin the triangle revealed by his undone collar and his strong forearms framed by rolled-up sleeves.

"Here." He crowds me against the desk, grabbing my thighs and lifting me while distracting me with a deep kiss.

There's a crash.

I turn just in time to see him sweeping everything off his desk, including a very expensive computer.

"Vito!" He takes my hands from where I'm holding his shoulders and lays me back. "What about—"

"Doesn't matter." He's on his knees, gripping my thigh and throwing it over his shoulder, before I can say more, his mouth is licking up my sex. I cry out, putty in his hands. "Fucking delicious," he tells me before licking me as though it's his religion.

I close my eyes and give in. I haven't touched myself all weekend. Since he made me come the urge has awakened, tingling even as I've been sad. But all that has been washed away and all that's left is sheer need.

"Give it to me." The demand is muffled by the fact he doesn't move his lips from my folds. "Come for me."

I nod frantically, even though Vito has his head between my legs, and can't see. He's licking with an intensity I'd have never believed if you'd told me only a few days ago. I need this man, and he needs me. My body knows this feeling now, and reaches for it, or rather, accepts what he pushes me into. Pleasure.

His tongue is different from his fingers from the other night, softer but no less determined. More so, perhaps, because he doesn't ease me into this slowly as he did on Friday night. It's a chase, and he's powerful and quick. I'm no match for him, and I claw at the table as the pressure mounts faster than I could have believed.

"Vito," I choke out. "I'm going to..."

"Now." He shoves a finger into my passage, and I scream. I split on that finger, my orgasm shuddering through me, the light of morning staining my eyelids and refusing to be dark as I convulse.

"That's it. Good girl." His voice rumbles into my bones as he eases me down from the peak. "Amore mio dolce."

"What does that mean?" I ask as I open my eyes. I gasp as I find him over me, his wet tongue replaced with the shift of his fine fabric hips on my inner thighs.

"My sweet love." He has his hands on either side of my head, and when he rocks against me his erection rubs hard over my clit, causing heat to flare up again. "It means my sweet love."

His sweet love? The endearment soaks into my skin, seeping into my heart. He called me that plenty of times on Friday. It feels warm and true.

Holding himself effortlessly on one hand, he reaches down and in seconds has freed his cock. Framed by his clothes, it's intimidating. Long and thick, with a vein pulsing and a bead of moisture on the tip that makes my mouth water.

And makes me tremble with both need and something like fear.

He's huge.

He angles his length and touches that throbbing, silky tip to where I'm aching for him.

"I need you now."

I nod eagerly. This is all my dreams come true. He wants me. He's turned on, and while he was a gentleman on Friday night, today he's feral. The evidence of his desire slowly breaches me, stealing my breath.

"That's it," he murmurs and lowers to press a kiss to my mouth. "Take my cock. Take it all."

Grabbing his shoulders, his muscles are warm and firm beneath my fingers as the sharp pinch eases, until he pushes again, and it hurts in the best way as he opens me up.

"You're being such a good girl for me."

"Make me yours," I plead against his lips, grappling with him, holding his shoulders and wrapping my legs around his waist until I realise leaving them wider gets him deeper. I don't care that it stings. I need him inside me. I want to be filled by him. "Please, Vito. Please."

"I'm going to look after you so well. You'll be utterly delirious with pleasure every moment of your life." He withdraws and slides back in, filling me even more. I'm stretched, and my god he's so big. I love it.

"Hush, hush. Breathe. You have to breathe through it." Vito strokes my cheek and it's only then I hear the unearthly noise from my throat. "Nearly there. I've got you."

Another withdrawal and I miss him immediately, but then the swollen head of his cock is at my entrance, and he feels so good as he drives far deeper this time. Until I can feel him under my ribs, and he pulls me up, wrapping one arm around my waist and the other my shoulders and kissing me so my head is forced back by his assault. His thick, long cock is wedged right in, and his hips are flush with mine, our chests pressed together from pelvis to neck.

"That's it, amore mio dolce," he murmurs against my lip. "That's it. You have everything now. Such a good girl. You've done it."

Then, he begins to move, holding me to him. I dig my fingers into the muscles on either side of his spine, because he feels incredible. He kisses me dominantly, his tongue in my mouth, as he starts slow. His hips piston forward and backwards with more speed, spiralling the pleasure higher with every movement of his hardness into where I'm soft to receive him.

His chest is pressed into mine, and just his hips are moving, him thrusting into me with a solid rhythm as he groans and shakes. This is the most intimate thing I've ever done in my life.

"You feel so good."

I haven't got the voice to reply. He's overwhelming. Pleasure swirls where we join. Each stroke of his body into mine feels like we're more together. More in sync. He moves like he can't get close enough.

I press my face into his neck, the dark stubble rough on my lips as I kiss him. My legs wrapped around him, I inhale his citrus and man scent, and wriggle my hips to try to get him deeper.

"Are you close to coming again?" he pants into my neck, sounding a bit on edge.

"I don't think so," I confess in a whisper. I didn't think women came just from sex? Those memes show women as really complicated, and while this is delicious and tingly and wonderful, it's not the same tension as when Vito made me come. "But you take what you need. Come inside me."

He groans incoherently, and then sucks in air, drawing back and looking me in the eyes. My in-control boss is back. "That won't do, Cassie. I need you to come on my cock, even if it takes until the sun sets. I'll wait, and fuck you until then."

"But I'm good! I've already come!" I protest as he peels my hands off his back and lays me back onto the desk, spread out, and the cool air hits my nipples, making them pinch.

"I won't breed you until you come for me."

10

VITO

I flex my hips, thrusting into Cassie with deliberate slowness, watching her face and feeling for the exact spot that drives her wild. The only difficulty is that she's so fucking perfect, I'm struggling to control myself and not pound into her recklessly. She's a virgin, I remind myself as I grab her thighs and push them wider.

She lets out a little involuntary mew as I angle my hips at the top of the stroke.

"Oh yeah, you like that, huh?" I murmur, and the way her eyes go hazy is the best reward for not totally losing it. I reach down to find her clit with my thumb, but make the mistake of shifting my gaze, and the sight of her pussy taking my cock makes me groan.

"You look so good. Pink, and slick, opening for your demanding boss."

She cranes her neck, trying to push up onto her elbows, her brows pinching.

"I can't see." She scowls a little and tries to bend more. "If I..."

"That won't work." But simultaneous to those words,

I'm affronted on her behalf that anatomy is such that she can't enjoy the sheer hotness of her pussy taking my cock as I fuck her. Shocking miscalculation by nature. "But this will."

"No!" she protests as I pull out.

"It's okay, this is going to be even better." I rub her lower abdomen with my palm in reassurance and a silent promise of what I'm going to put there. A baby. "Do you trust me?"

"Yes." And her big soft-blue eyes are full of belief that makes my chest swell with love. My perfect girl.

"Stay there," I order. "Don't move."

I find the window control on the floor next to the computer, which miraculously both seem to be unbroken, and flick the button to turn the glass into a mirror.

"What are you doing?" Cassie sounds a bit uncertain.

"Giving you the beautiful view you deserve, amore mio dolce."

I grab the sofa and drag it over to the partially-opaque window, my cock bobbing as I do so. Then, from her discarded purse and my suit jacket, I find our phones. Cassie blinks at me, confused as I place them on the sofa.

"But you've just blocked the view." This time her tone is confused, and almost frustrated. Understandable, since her poor little clit will be throbbing with unfulfilled need.

Striding over, I grin. "I've just enabled the best view of all."

The window is a huge mirror now. Lifting her is easy, and in a second, I've set her onto the sofa.

"Get on your hands and knees," I command, and she scrambles to obey. "Look straight ahead. Into the mirror."

Standing behind her as I strip off my clothes is heaven. She's utterly beautiful, watching my reflection with her eyes wide open. Her gaze is everywhere, taking in my arms and pecs then following the trail of dark hair down my chest to where my cock juts upwards.

That part of me is very enthusiastic about the turn of events that means I get to see more as I fuck her, and as well as still glistening with her juices, pre-come is beading at the tip.

Naked, on all fours, she's temptation incarnate, and I'm done resisting.

"Push your arse back and your tits forward." It's a filthy command made in a gruff voice that's probably too much for my little virgin girl.

But a whimper escapes her open lips, and she arches into me. In the mirror, her tits are on show, her hair falling over her shoulder. There are so many lovely parts of her to look at, but her arse and wet cunt are so exposed like this, and I take a moment to admire them. Then I run a possessive hand from between her shoulder blades down her back and over the curve of her arse.

She's as fresh and ripe as a peach, and I'm a forty-year-old man who has made a career of being the worst person in Milan, and now London. The mirror tells me I have lines around my eyes and silver in my hair. I don't deserve her.

And I don't care. I'm going to have her in every way.

I settle one knee onto the sofa, and ruthlessly shove her legs further apart. She gasps. Taking my cock in my hand, and watching her face in the mirror, I rub the head up and down her drenched slit, then slide back into her. Home. As I look into her soft eyes, and her hot, wet, welcoming pussy accommodates my length, I know I'm where I'm meant to be.

"So tight," I murmur. "You feel amazing."

Cassie's gaze flits between my face and my chest, impaling herself further on my shaft. I grip her hips and give a few languid strokes, ensuring I hit that magic place on her inner walls that's connected to her clit, before building up a rhythm.

"It's different...from this angle." Her voice hitches as I bottom out against the entrance to her womb. "You look..." She can't seem to find the words, just squirming on my cock as she stares at me. A thrill of ownership flares in me that she might never have seen a real man naked before.

"Enjoying the mirror?" I thrust into her.

She swallows, then nods helplessly.

"Now." I pick up my phone and a smirk tugs at my lips as her brow creases in confusion again even as she moans when I hit deep inside her then draw back out languorously. "Answer the video call."

"What?" The word is breathy.

I hit the call button, and a second later Cassie has pulled her phone to her and accepted.

"Ciao, bella," I croon and tap to turn the camera around. Then I move it to capture the place where I'm breaching her. "Look at your sweet little pink pussy. Look how you're opening for me."

"Oh, my!"

Glancing in the mirror, I grin as I see her transfixed by the screen.

There are so many good views. The slick folds of her sex enveloping my cock. Her back, the curve of her hip, and her little arse too. Her smooth skin. But what I enjoy most—the biggest turn-on for me—is Cassie's face as she sees us join. I bet she's never even seen how pretty she is down there.

"That's really you and me," she says wonderingly, gaping at the screen. "That's what you see?"

"I see my good girl." I withdraw then pull her back onto

my cock gradually, both of us watching me fill her inch by inch. My hardness slides into where she's soft and wet. "Taking everything I've got."

I do it again, ignoring my body's demand to take her hard and fast and finish deep inside her. To breed her with hot spurts of come.

"No more secrets. No more concealment."

"You're beautiful."

And I smile at her description of me when she's the beautiful one. I increase my pace. Fucking her faster and deeper as pleasure spins through me.

She's gripping the screen between her hands now, head tilting up and down to get the whole vision of me above her in the mirror, and how I'm sliding into her on our live video call. "I need to see this again when—mmmm—you're not *distracting* me."

I laugh. "Amore mio dolce, I'm going to want to do this every single day, with or without as many mirrors and cameras and kinky toys. I will never get enough of your sweet body." Letting go of her hip, I alter the angle of my phone and reach down to find her clit with my fingers. "Because you're more beautiful and feel better around my cock than all I've experienced in forty years, or ever will. I'm going to keep you."

"Ohhh..." She lets out a long, breathy moan as I circle over her clit. "This is beyond anything I've ever imagined."

"It'll be even better every time," I promise as I slide in and out of her at an easy pace so she can fully enjoy the view of her pussy and me fingering her. "I'm going to treat you like a princess."

Working circles over her clit, I murmur words of praise and love as she begins to shake. She's so pretty as she struggles to keep herself together.

"Fuck, Cassie. I love you so much. I can't wait to do this when you're pregnant."

Her chin snaps up and there's shock in her eyes as she stares at me in the mirror. "What?"

"I'm going to get you pregnant, you know that," I reply.

"I thought it was a joke."

"Not even slightly." I ram into her, hard, and she jolts with the power of it. "Right here. I'm going to spill all my seed against your womb, and breed you."

She squeaks, and her gaze dips to the video that I'm still streaming between our phones.

"Want to see it all?" I tighten my grip on her hip and pull slowly out, all the way until the head pops out, slick with her juices. "Look at all that cream. You made it just for me. To ease my way to breeding you. The next time we do this it will be with all my come inside you. Such a messy girl." Then I push back in, one aching inch at a time.

"You really want us to have babies?" She gasps out.

The tip of my cock tingles. "There's a reason we're not using a condom. I want you to be my wife, have my children, and be thoroughly loved and spoiled and cared for."

It's difficult to say in words how much I adore her, so I show her. I switch to short, intense thrusts of just the tip of me into her, setting both of us alight where we're most sensitive. I rock into her, then draw out to long, deep thrusts that feel even better. I'm inside her, and fuck it feels so good. Amazing.

"Vito." Her eyes drift closed in bliss.

"Watch," I insist, and her eyes fly open again. "Don't stop looking. We're making every second of this count. I'll never take you for the first time again. You won't be my horny little virgin again."

Her whimper is the sweetest thing I've ever heard.

"Look at how pretty you are. It makes me hard as fuck that I'm raw inside you. Nothing between us."

I take a risk and pinch her clit. "Come for me."

She screams as she breaks, squeezing my cock. Her head thrown back, her berry-nipple tipped breasts in the mirror, her sweet, peachy arse naked and her back curved, she's more gorgeous than I could have believed possible as she comes all over my cock. She tenses around my length and the surge of pleasure is enhanced by the triumph that my virgin girl is coming for me.

I drop the phone, grab her, and unleash all my base instincts. I fuck her hard and deep. She feels too good. Made for me.

The steady pace I've established goes erratic. I tighten my grip on her soft arse and pound into her, finally allowing myself to use her. I chase my orgasm, and she's my pliant girl as she recovers from the first of many, many orgasms she'll have while I breed her.

"Mine," I growl as pleasure pools at the base of my spine. Every slam of my cock into her feels better and better. "I'm going to give you everything."

"Yes. Please. Please." She holds my gaze in the mirror and pleasure surges over me. However much I wanted this time to last forever, my orgasm overcomes me, as inevitable as the dawn and just as awe-inspiring. I hold her flush to me, joining as closely as possible. The pleasure is so good it's almost painful as I shoot into her, filling her up.

The orgasm she gives me is so intense I can hardly make my muscles work. I fall back onto the cushions, bringing Cassie with me so she ends up in my lap, me still embedded deep in her.

We recover like that for a long time.

I kiss her shoulder, and her neck. I stroke all the parts of her I can get to and make her tuck closer so I can reach her calves. Her toes. I whisper words of love and the sensation of her skin on mine convinces me this is real in a way nothing else could. She's unimaginably soft.

"Hold it in, Cassie," I tell her when I slide out of her pussy. "Don't waste it."

Clasping between her legs, she looks up at me, naughty and happy and content and I kiss her mouth again and again.

I don't notice the absence of the tightness that's been in my chest for so long immediately, only the relief. There's something physically different about being with the woman I love.

Eventually, reality intrudes. We'd been ignoring the sounds of admin assistants arriving, but my office phone rings.

"Should we...?" Cassie asks tentatively.

"No."

"Vito! We have to move eventually!" She wriggles.

"We don't. Questa è la nostra casa. This is our home now. This office. We're never leaving."

And when Cassie snuggles back onto my chest, I can almost believe that's true. Until the phone rings again. On the fifth time, I sigh.

I shift her onto the sofa and leave her there, walking naked to my clear desk and kneel to pick up the phone from the mess on the floor.

"I'm not here for the rest of the day, or tomorrow. Neither is Cassie Meadows. Don't ring again unless..." There's spluttering on the other end of the phone as I take a moment to consider what could be as important as Cassie. "It's the literal end of the world and I am the only person who can save it."

Replacing the phone, I notice something I'd forgotten next to the pens and broken keyboard.

"I was going to ask you something before you tried to quit." I pick up the box and return to where Cassie is still holding my come in her pussy like a good girl.

I return to her, and sink to one knee. Opening the velvet box towards her, I watch her beautiful face blank with surprise as she realises what I'm doing and gasps.

"Marry me."

The ring is excessive. I bought it over the weekend, torn apart by love and despair and hope. It's a pale-blue sapphire the colour of her eyes, set in a platinum band.

"Yes." She grins, propels herself forwards, grips me with both hands as she nods and hides her face in my shoulder. "Yes. Always, yes."

EPILOGUE
CASSIE

Five years later

"It's ridiculous," says Anwyn. "The heroine is too stupid to live." She waves her paperback copy of the romance book we've all been reading for the London Mafia Smut Club.

"You're being way too harsh." Jenna Voronov shakes her head. "People don't make perfect decisions in the heat of the moment. They don't think of other things that might be obvious in hindsight."

"Yes!" Lina says, pulling out her eReader. "See, I agree with Jenna. Listen to this bit." And proceeds to read aloud about the part where the heroine of the fantasy romance is riding a dragon to get to her enemy or friend or lover, depending on where abouts in the book you are and how you look at it. "Not stupid. At all. She's in love."

"At that point?" Anwyn scoffs. "Too early, see she says—"

"Unreliable narrator." Lina shrugs happily. "She loves him, just doesn't know it.

I don't get involved with these arguments. Ella Blackwood and I tend to hang out on the same sofa and watch with amusement as the more opinionated members get involved. The funniest times are when some of the husbands read along, and join in the debate. Lambeth and Mayfair once nearly came to blows about a disagreement over the realism of a cowboy romance.

One of the advantages of being the wife of a mafia boss is the club. You'd think that the London Mafia was all rivalry and drive-by shootings, and sure, there is still some argument with the Greek mafias that I haven't fully understood.

But when I stepped into the bar on the night Vito and I got together, I longed for family and friends. I remember looking at the group of women and being jealous I didn't have that. Now, I have Vito, our two daughters, Gabriella and Isabella, and as much female companionship as I like with the other London Mafia Syndicate wives.

"I know we're supposed to be talking about the book," whispers Ella next to me, "but do you want to go to the waterpark next Saturday? I was thinking of taking the kids."

"Sure," I reply. You'd think that hanging out with the wife of a man who looks almost identical to your husband would be awkward, but Ella and Sev's wife have become some of my best friends. And the three Blackwood triplets are easy to distinguish if one of them is your lover. I'd know Vito anywhere.

"Am I invited?" a sinfully delicious voice rumbles behind us, then bristles rasp on my cheek. "I love wet fun," Vito murmurs into my ear, low enough that only I hear.

I flush and look up at my husband. He gives my hair a playful tug and leans down to kiss me. It's a soft and lingering kiss, not filthy and open-mouthed, but a clear enough sign of possession. His lips on mine make a thought rise in me again that I've been having more and more, recently.

I think I'd like to be pregnant again. I'd like my husband to breed me. I want that solid, rounded belly that Vito can't keep his hands off.

Well. Even more than usual. My husband is happiest when we're touching.

He draws back and drags his gaze over my face and shoulders in a carnal sweep so hot I'm instantly chargrilled.

"Ready to go back to our brood?" he asks, smiling.

I swear I thought I was marrying a black cloud. But nope. My husband is pure sunshine about... Okay, only about fifty per cent of the time. And he's the best with the kids. He has infinite patience for everything they want to do, and every mistake.

"Yes. Let's go." We are total home-bodies, even if we have homes all over the world. London, Milan, a villa in Naples and another in the south of Italy, but also New York, Bali, and South Africa.

Tonight though, we slide into the car that will take us back to the house in London where it all started, and our babies are sleeping under the supervision of their Italian nanny.

Vito pulls me onto his lap in the car.

"You're my lovely girl." He strokes my hair, and I tip my head into his touch.

"My husband." I'm not sure how to broach the topic of another child.

"My wife."

He examines me, and while I can't see the colour of his eyes in the dark back of the car, I can tell he's looking at me. It sends a warm shiver down my spine, even now after so many years. He's still incredibly handsome, and I am still not over the shock that he's mine.

And I want to have more of his babies. Two is not enough.

"What is it, amore mio dolce?" he asks softly. "You look concerned."

"Can we have another baby?"

"That's what you worried about asking?" He huffs out a laugh and shakes his head. "Si. Always yes, for you."

"Really? You said you needed more sleep?"

"I love losing sleep to our babies." He strokes the back of my neck. "Even if I grumble. Nothing will ever be as good as filling you up with seed and showing you how I love you, over and over." Pulling me closer, he slides his hand down until it finds the hem of my silk dress. "Let's start tonight."

I melt and breathe in his familiar citrus and sandalwood scent like I'm an addict. I am. I can never get enough of Vito.

"And in the office, tomorrow," he adds. "Over my desk."

EXTENDED EPILOGUE
VITO

"Mr Blackwood?"

I look up to find my wife at my office door, wearing a dress I don't recognise. It's silky, with a flirty hem and is the bright blue of our children's eyes. Cassie steals my breath in everything she wears, but this dress instantly hardens my cock.

"I'm here about the job, sir," Cassie adds, and I have to look down at my desk to hide my smile.

We're playing that game, are we?

"Come in," I say when I've composed myself. I look up and rake my gaze over her. She's utterly gorgeous. My mouth waters. "Close the door behind you."

The sounds of the rest of the office are silenced as she walks across to my desk, generous hips swaying.

"So..."

"I know I'm not qualified for the role," she blurts out. "But I'm really keen. I'm a hard worker."

"Are you indeed?" I lower my brows, like I used to when I was irritated that she wasn't looking after herself as she ought before we were married. It's never an issue now. I take care of everything. Cassie might be co-CEO, but I'm frequently so busy with the less-legal and more mafia parts of my empire that she is the real power in this room. Which is ironic, because she gives me big blue doe-eyes.

"Anything, Mr Blackwood. I'll do anything you say."

I shove my chair back and crook my finger. "Come here."

"Around the desk?" Cassie says, with the perfect amount of horny reluctance, as though she's still my virgin employee.

"Yes, around the desk. Show me what you'll do."

Her pretty mouth falls open but she obeys as eagerly and seductively as might be expected, given this is her scene. She deliberately swings her hips more than usual, and I swear she's pushing out her spectacular tits.

"Such a fucking little tease," I growl and she gasps. "A perfect actress, aren't you? Coming in here saying you want a job, when actually you want something else, don't you?"

Cassie bites her lip and looks at me coyly, playing with the hem of her dress, tugging it up her thighs just a few tantalising inches. "I don't know what you mean..."

"Si. You do, bella. Tell me what you want like a good girl, and I'll give it to you."

"I heard that you're a good boss, and a good man..."

"Oh, did you now? Go on."

She blushes so prettily. "I hoped you could..."

"Hmmhum," I prompt her, keeping my expression serious.

"I want to get pregnant," she whispers.

I raise one eyebrow. "You want me to fill you up with my seed, make you swollen with my child, then look after you and the baby?" As I say that, I reach out and stroke a possessive hand over her belly. "You want everyone to know that the mafia boss fucked you?"

She squirms. "Would you?"

"Maybe if you're ready for me." I take my hand from her and palm my now achingly hard cock. "And you'll need to know two things."

"What's that?" Her chest is pink and she is breathing fast. Fuck she's so lovely when she's aroused. I love this woman more than life itself.

"Turn around, and lean over the desk, and I'll tell you."

Her eyebrows twitch down. "Don't—"

"Don't tell me what to do if you want me to give you a baby," I growl. "Turn around."

Reluctantly, she turns, and I allow myself a silent laugh. She wanted to tell me not to push anything off the desk. Amore mio dulce worries about these things.

"Lie on the desk."

She slowly lowers herself so her generous tits are laid on my piles of paperwork.

"Good. Now lift your skirt."

I watch, entranced, as she raises that flirty little sundress and reveals her naked skin. I groan. "You little slut. You didn't wear any knickers so I could rail you, huh?"

"Yes," she whispers.

My cock is throbbing. I release it with shaky hands, shoving down my trousers only just enough.

"You want my cock in this little pussy?" I ask, moving so I'm standing behind her.

"Please." Her voice is high.

"You want me to fill you with come?" I pitch my voice lower, in contrast to hers. I know my deep gruff tone makes her heated and needy. "Make you pregnant?"

It's a whine this time.

"I will. I promise I will. But you should know, amore mio dolce: I'm not a good man. I'm a possessive tyrant who once I've filled you with my come is going to own you, body and soul. I'll use your body and give you a baby, but you'll never escape me."

She shudders and my smile broadens.

I cup her bottom and squeeze, then slap her arse cheek just enough to sting in the best way, which forces a squeak to escape her.

"Open your legs," I demand. "Show me your pussy."

She obeys instantly this time, and her beautiful pink folds are revealed. All slick and plump and needy. I run my finger up the centre and she moans.

"That's such a good welcome." Her slit is soaking. "This hot, wet pussy is begging to be filled isn't it?"

She nods and spreads her legs further.

I grab my cock and give it a few pumps with my hand, a grunt of desire and anticipation tearing from my throat as I then touch the head to her folds. "I'm going to fuck a baby into this perfect body of yours. I'm going to use you, and breed you. You want that?"

"Yes," she admits. "Yes."

My hips flex forwards and I breach her. "You're so sexy."

"Put a baby in me." She squirms on the first inch of my cock.

"Take it all," I groan as I slide all the way to the hilt, so easy because she's soaking. "Oh fuck." I have to still when I'm entirely in her. Not because she needs time to adjust—no, I've had her enough times she can do that no problem now—but because the way she squeezes me makes my heart palpitate every time.

"I'm so full of your cock," she murmurs, hands gripping the papers on my desk.

"That's my little slut of a wife," I say in Italian. "My beautiful girl." Then I grin, because right on cue, Cassie moans. She loves it when I speak dirty to her in Italian.

Beginning to thrust, I reach up and gather her hair, wrapping it around my fist as I increase my pace.

"More," she pants. "Deeper. Please Vito, I need you."

"You're like a bitch in heat, aren't you," I croon and she whimpers, pushing back onto my cock eagerly.

I press one hand between her shoulder blades, holding her in place as though she doesn't want this. As though she isn't keeping her hips lifted so I can fuck her, and arching her back so her nipples rub on the desk. I take her hard and fast, ramming into her. I use her pussy, just as I said. I don't hold back. I slam our bodies together until she's crying out, moaning and writhing with pleasure and I don't think I can take much more without exploding.

"Want me to get you pregnant again, little whore?"

"Yes," she moans. "Come inside me. Please." And then it's my turn to not be able to contain how much I want this.

My thrusts speed up, going erratic. My cock feels like it might explode.

"Come for me then, slut. Milk it out of me." My voice is hoarse with emotion and pure lust. I love this woman so much. I'd do anything for her. "Make me give you a baby."

She tightens around my cock and I groan.

"Like that?" she asks, all innocent.

I grip her even harder, and slam into her. The way she has constricted around my shaft makes it almost difficult to get in, despite how slick she is, and I grunt as I ram in, over and over. But fuck, it feels amazing when she's so tight like this.

Letting out a stream of filthy words in Italian, my balls pull up, ready, as she squirms. "Give it to me, husband. Harder."

"Do you like that you might get pregnant from my cock?"

Reaching around, I stroke her clit and she whines, instantly clenching around my cock.

"Milk it," I encourage her. "Get what you need from my cock, my little come-slut. Are you desperate for my come?"

I feel her nod more than see. My vision is going hazy.

"Please," she begs. "Please."

"I love it when you beg." Because fuck, I would beg her every day for the privilege of having her like this. "And I love using your pussy like this. Breeding you."

Rubbing her exactly the way she likes it is instinct now, and she's close as I keep slamming into her.

"That's my good girl. Such a good fucking girl for me. Come on my cock."

A firm pinch on her clit and she does exactly as I said, and drags me into orgasm with her, milking me.

"You're mine now. All mine." I grit out the possessive words as ecstasy overtakes my whole body, wracking through me from where we're joined all the way to my fingertips and toes.

I collapse onto my forearms over my wife and kiss her cheek until she giggles and stretches around so our lips meet.

"I love you," she says between kisses. "I love you so much. Thank you for the baby."

And hell, my poor heart can't take it. I'm the luckiest man in London to have such a perfect sweet wife. "Amore mio dolce."

Printed in Dunstable, United Kingdom